Whoops! Our New Flatmate Is A Human

Published by Implode Publishing Ltd
© Implode Publishing Ltd 2016

The right of Adele Abbott to be identified as the Author
of the Work has been asserted by her in accordance with
the Copyright, Designs and Patents Act 1988.

Chapter 1

"You must be the new girl." The man perched on Susan Hall's desk had a comb-over and bad breath.

"And you are?" She pushed her chair back in an attempt to get out of halitosis range.

"Dougal Andrews."

"I thought so."

"You've heard of me, then?" He smiled a nicotine smile. "Nice to know my reputation precedes me. How are you settling in?"

"So far, so good." She checked her watch. "But then it is only ten past nine, and this is my first day."

"A bunch of us usually go to the Walrus and Hammer at lunchtime. Why don't you join us? We could do with a pretty face."

Susan wasn't about to argue with that sentiment. Dougal Andrews could definitely have done with a prettier face.

"Thanks, but I'll have to pass. I'm not much of a drinker."

"That'll soon change, after you've been here a few weeks." He grinned. "What are you working on?"

"Nothing much." She clicked the mouse to minimise the window on her computer screen. "I've got a meeting with the boss in five minutes."

"The boss? You mean Fat Freddy? I wouldn't take much notice of him. We're the ones who keep this boat afloat."

"We?"

"Me and the other reporters. If it wasn't for us, this place would have sunk years ago."

"Interesting." She stood up, hoping that he'd take the

hint.

"Yeah. So, like I said, we'll be in the Walrus from about midday. Try and make it. You'll brighten the place up."

Susan watched Dougal saunter back to his desk, cracking jokes with his male colleagues as he went. She couldn't hear what he said, but would have bet her first month's salary that she was the butt of them. She felt a little dirty, but wasn't sure if that was the result of her encounter with Dougal, or the shower in that flea-pit of a motel she was holed up in. It had been on the blink that morning. Again.

***

"Mr Flynn?" Susan knocked on the already open door.

"Come in. Push the door closed behind you, would you?" He waited until the door clicked to. "Please call me Flynn."

"Sure."

"I see you've met Dougal Andrews."

"Just now."

"He's one of the reasons I hired you. The other reasons will be with him in the Walrus at lunchtime."

"He invited me to join them for a drink."

"What did you say?"

"That I don't drink."

"You're teetotal?"

"No. I just don't drink with men like Dougal Andrews."

"I inherited this crowd of no-hopers." He gestured to the outer office. "My predecessor had very low standards when it came to recruitment criteria. If they could spell their name, and were prepared to stand him a drink, he'd hire them. You're *my* first recruit, and hopefully the foundation of the new Bugle. To tell you the truth, I was a little surprised when you accepted the job offer."

"I like a challenge."

"Just as well because the future of this newspaper may well depend on our ability to turn it around."

"No pressure, then?"

"There'll be lots of pressure. That much I can promise you. Pressure from me, pressure from the new owners who want this newspaper's reputation restored, and pressure from Dougal and his drinking buddies who will do everything they can to resist change. Think you're up to it?"

"I'll give it my best shot."

As Susan made her way back to her desk, one of the other reporters stood up, and deliberately blocked her way. The man was fat, ugly, and had sweat patches under both of his arms. A real catch.

"While you're on your feet, why don't you make me a cup of tea." He held out a mug which was already stained brown. "I like plenty of milk and a couple of sugars. Oh, and check if we've got any biscuits. If not, be a good girl and nip to the shop next door to buy some digestives."

"If you want a cup of tea, I suggest you make one yourself. I'm not here to make drinks for you or anyone else. Now, if you wouldn't mind getting out of my way."

The man stepped to one side, but left only just enough room for her to squeeze past. As she did, he gave her a light tap on her backside.

Susan spun around, grabbed his arm, pushed it up his back, and slammed him face down onto the desk.

"Let me go!"

"If you ever lay another finger on me, I will rip off your hands, and feed them to you. Do you understand?"

"Okay. Okay. It was only a joke. Let me go! That hurts."

"Did you hear what I said?"

"Yes. I'm sorry. Let me go. Please!"

When she released her grip, there were tears in the man's eyes, and his nose was running. As she made her way back to her desk, her heart was racing. Behind her, she could hear a dozen whispering voices.

This was going to be a very long week.

Later that morning, she was in the ladies' room when another young woman came in. Susan had noticed her earlier, sitting at the far end of the office. Her red hair was in a bob, and she looked as though she'd have trouble saying boo to a goose.

"Hi." Susan smiled. "I'm sorry, I don't know your name."

"Stella. Stella Yates."

"I'm Susan Hall."

"Yes, I know. I hope you don't mind my saying, but I thought what you did out there was fantastic."

"You mean to the fat guy?"

"Yeah. That's Bob Bragg. He's been asking for that for ages. Where did you learn that stuff?"

"I have three older brothers. Two of them are into martial arts; the other is a boxer. I did both—just so I could kick all of their asses. What do you do here, Stella?"

"I'm one of the admin assistants, but really I'm just a dogsbody—like all the other women in this office. The men think we're only here to make tea and coffee, and run their errands. I wouldn't mind so much if they would just ask nicely. And, they're always trying it on like Bob did with you."

"You shouldn't put up with it."

"I know, but I can't afford to lose this job."

"If anyone does anything like that to you again, come and talk to me."

"I don't want to get into trouble."

"You won't. I promise. Just come and tell me, and I'll sort it."

***

"Can you tell me who looks after the classified ads?" Susan said.

She was on the floor above her own—in advertising sales. The huge room, which was much noisier than the newsroom, was a hive of activity as the sales team made phone call after phone call in a desperate bid to hit their target, and make that month's bonus. It was a certain breed of person who sold display ads. Susan had encountered them before in her previous job. The men all had slicked-back hair, and used way too much aftershave. The women spent half their bonus on makeup.

"You want Carly." The man pointed to a desk in the far corner of the room.

As Susan zigzagged her way through the rows of desks, her senses were assaulted by a dozen different perfumes and aftershaves.

"Carly?"

The woman looked up from her computer screen. Carly was a mouse in an office full of hungry cats.

"Yes?"

"I'm Susan Hall. I've just started here today."

"Oh, hi. I didn't know they were taking on any more sales people."

"I'm actually a reporter—from the floor below."

"Oh, right. I wouldn't like to work with that lot downstairs. This crowd are bad enough, but at least they keep their hands to themselves. Most of them anyway."

"I wanted to ask you a favour."

"What's that?"

"I'm living out of a suitcase in a motel just outside of Washbridge. I desperately need to find a flat-share, but every time I see something that looks even half decent, it's already been snapped up. I was just wondering if you could give me the nod if you get any flat-share ads. That way, I can get the jump on them before they're published."

"Of course. What's your extension number?"

***

When Susan had been interviewed for the job by Flynn, he'd told her that he wanted someone who could bring in the 'big' stories. The Bugle had a reputation, which stretched far beyond Washbridge, for being a sleazy rag not much better than the average gossip magazine. When its new owners had taken control, one of the first things they had done was to sack the previous editor-in-chief. Flynn, who had built a solid reputation at a publication in the north, had been their first appointment; Susan was his. There were many reasons why she'd taken the job, some of which she hadn't shared with Flynn. The challenge of bringing in the 'big' stories had certainly been a major draw. Now all she had to do was deliver.

"Hey, Suzy!" Dougal called from down the office. "There's someone here who'd like a word with you."

Dougal walked a woman across the room to Susan's desk.

"There you go, Margie. This young lady will look after you from now on, won't you Suzy?"

Susan could tell by the smirk on Dougal's face that she wasn't going to like this, but she offered the woman a chair.

"Hi, I'm Susan Hall. Dougal said you were Margie?"

"Margie Redflower."

"Is there something I can help you with, Margie?"

"It's the usual."

Susan glanced down the room. Dougal, Bob and three other men were congregated by the water cooler. They were all looking her way, and laughing.

"What exactly is the 'usual'? I only started here today, so I—"

"The wizards."

"Wizards?"

"And witches."

"Witches?"

"And all the others."

"I'm sorry. I'm not sure I follow."

"I've told him all this before." She pointed to Dougal, who was clearly enjoying Susan's predicament. "But he hasn't done anything about it."

They'd had their fair share of nutjobs at Susan's previous newspaper. The tinfoil hat brigade with their conspiracy theories and UFO sightings. It looked like

Dougal had passed on Washbridge's version to her.

"I'm not familiar with your story, Margie. Maybe you should start at the beginning."

"My husband, Gary, disappeared two years ago. They took him."

"They?"

"Rogue Retrievers. That's what Gary used to call them."

"Rogue what?"

"Retrievers. They're from Candlefield."

"Is that close by?" Susan had thought she knew all the local towns and villages.

"It's in the supernatural world."

It was at precisely that moment that Susan decided she was going to have a serious talk to Dougal Andrews after she'd managed to get rid of crazy Margie.

"The Rogue Retrievers are sent to take back sups who have broken the rules."

"Sorry? Did you say sups?"

"Yes—supernaturals." Margie sighed, obviously exasperated at having to explain the whole thing again. "They took Gary back."

"To Candlefield?"

"Yes. Because he'd told me he was a wizard. That's why they did it."

"When did he tell you? That he was a wizard, I mean?"

"A few years after we were married. But I'd already guessed something wasn't right before then."

"How do you mean?"

"I'd caught him doing magic."

"Card tricks? That sort of thing?"

"No. Real magic. One day, he turned next door's dog into a statue because it was making too much noise."

"And you actually saw this?"

"Yes. He didn't know I was there. He turned it straight back, but I'd already seen it."

"Right. And, you haven't seen Gary since he was — err — retrieved?"

"That's right."

"What about the police?"

"They reckon he must have left of his own accord."

"Did you tell them about the — err — wizard thing?"

"Of course, but they just think I'm crazy. Everyone does."

"Right."

"What about you? Do you think I'm crazy too?"

"I'd like to think I have an open-mind."

"Will you look into it? This could be a big story."

And probably the last one she'd ever write. "I'll certainly give it some serious thought, but it is my first day in the job, so it might be a while before I get around to it."

"I can bring you up to speed, if you like. I've got lots more information."

"Why don't you leave me your contact details, so I can get in touch with you?" Susan pushed a notepad and pen across the desk.

"This is big," Margie said, after she'd scribbled down her address and phone number.

"I can see that. I'll be in touch."

Before Margie was even out of the office, Dougal was standing at Susan's desk. "No need to thank me for the scoop."

"She needs professional help." Susan slid the notepad into the top drawer of her desk. "How long has she been coming in here with that same story?"

"Every month for the last two years." Dougal laughed. "It's good of you to offer to take it on."

Chapter 2

"Charlie!" Dorothy shouted from the kitchen area of the open-plan apartment.

"What? I'm busy."

"Come here."

Charlie hauled his huge frame off the sofa, and dragged himself over to where Dorothy was standing. "What's up?"

"Have you seen my blood?"

"Only that time when you'd been shaving your legs, and nicked one of them."

"Not *that* blood. I mean my synthetic blood. The stuff I drink. Are you even awake?"

"Not really. It was a full moon last night, remember?"

"Oh yeah. Sorry. Late night for you, I guess?"

"Yeah. Very."

"I put two litres of blood in here yesterday, but it's disappeared."

"Morning." Neil was wearing his Doobysaurus dressing gown and matching slippers.

"Neil, have you seen my blood?"

"Only that time you'd been shaving your legs, and—"

"She means the stuff she drinks," Charlie said.

"Oh, right. Yeah, I put it in the bread bin."

"In the bread bin?" Dorothy shook her head in disbelief. "Why?"

"None of us eats bread, so it was just standing empty."

"I don't mean why did you put it in *the bread bin*. I mean why did you take it out of the fridge in the first place?"

"It turns my stomach. Every time I open the fridge door—there it is. It put me right off my porridge yesterday."

"I thought we'd agreed." Dorothy sighed. "The top shelf of the fridge is Charlie's, the bottom shelf is yours, and the middle shelf is mine!"

"We did. But that was only for food. Not for—" He pulled a face. "You know—"

"You're allowed to say the word. It won't kill you. B-L-O-O-D. Blood!"

"Blood, yeah." Neil shuddered. "But, like I said, the fridge is just for food."

"That *is* my food."

"It's not really food though, is it? Not like fish and chips, or steak and onion pie?"

"It's real food to me. If I don't get a regular supply, I'll die."

"Aren't you dead already?"

"No—yes—well—sort of. But what does that matter? It doesn't give you the right to mess with my meals. If it makes you feel so queasy, why don't you cast a spell so you can't see it?"

"It's not like I threw it out. It's right there—in the bread bin."

"It's no good to me in there. I like my blood served cold."

"What we need," Charlie interrupted. "Is another fridge. One for food, and one for—err—other stuff."

"And who's going to pay for that?" Dorothy turned on him. "Not me. Have you forgotten we're six days late with this month's rent?"

"Ten." Charlie yawned. "It was due on the fifth. It's the fifteenth today."

Dorothy walked over to the bread bin, took out the two

bottles of synthetic blood, and put them on the middle shelf of the fridge.

"Just keep your hands off them!" She fixed Neil with her gaze.

"We never had this trouble with Ruth." Neil poured himself a bowl of cornflakes.

"That's because Ruth satisfied her hunger with human blood. You should be grateful I stick to synthetic. At least you know the Rogue Retrievers won't be hammering on our door at any moment."

"Talking of which," Charlie said. "I still don't understand why you two vetoed that Rogue Retriever who came to see the room last week."

"You do know what the Rogue Retrievers do, don't you?" Dorothy said.

"Of course I do. But it's not like any of us gets up to anything that would get us taken back to Candlefield, is it?"

"It would be like living on a knife-edge," Neil said.

"Just one wrong move, and 'Pow'," Dorothy said.

"Precisely! Pow!" Neil thumped the table. "Have you ever seen a Rogue Retriever in action?"

Charlie shook his head.

"I have." Neil tipped the bowl to his lips, and drank the last few drops of milk.

"Must you do that?" Dorothy pulled a face. "It's gross."

"That's the best bit. Like I was saying, I had a wizard friend who got caught by the Rs."

"Sounds painful." Charlie laughed. "What had he done, this friend of yours?"

"Nothing much. Just had a minor disagreement with a bookmaker."

"And?"

"And turned him into a frog. Or a toad. I never have been able to tell the difference. Anyway, along comes a Rogue Retriever—Daze, Taze or maybe Haze—some stupid name like that—and throws a net over poor old Billy. Pow! He disappeared. Never seen him since."

"If we don't find someone to take that fourth bedroom soon," Charlie said. "We'll all be out on our Rs."

"I don't understand why it's so difficult." Neil sighed.

"It's pretty obvious why," Dorothy said. "It's that stupid ghost of yours."

"I've told you before, Socky isn't my ghost." Neil added his bowl to the mountain of dishes.

"You're the one who invited him in here."

"I didn't realise *he* was a *he*. I thought it might be a pretty young female ghost."

"So why didn't you send him packing when you saw who he was?"

"It doesn't work like that. Once you've allowed a ghost to attach itself to you, it will only go away if *it* decides to."

"No one is going to rent that room with him in it," Dorothy said. "It's always freezing cold, and then there's the sound of him walking around on his peg leg."

"You have to try to persuade him to leave," Charlie said. "If we don't get that fourth room let soon, we'll all be out on the streets."

"Okay, but I'll just be wasting my time." Neil made his way to the fourth bedroom. As soon as he stepped inside, he felt the familiar chill. It was several degrees colder than the rest of the apartment.

"Socky!" He regretted the word as soon as it had left his lips.

A ghostly figure appeared in front of him. The man was dressed in a long drape coat. "My name, I'll remind you, is Tobias Fotheringham."

"Of course, Tobias. Sorry."

"Did you want something, young man?"

"We have a bit of a problem. We really need to let this room, so you'll have to move somewhere else."

The ghost laughed. "Young man, I'll have you know that I've been in this building since the early 1900s. I once owned this place. Have you forgotten that this building was home to Fotheringham Socks? The best socks in the country. And I was the wealthiest landowner around these parts. I could have bought and sold you a thousand times over."

"That's all very interesting, but that was a very long time ago. This is not a sock factory any more, in case you hadn't noticed."

"I've certainly noticed. After my fateful accident, I stayed in the factory to keep an eye on things. Things weren't always run as I would have liked, but at least socks were still being manufactured. But then, the place closed, and they did *this* to it. What is this building now anyway? What possible use is it to anyone?"

"These are apartments. People live here."

"*This* room is not an 'apartment.' This is my office, and has been for over a hundred years."

"But can't you see—it's no longer an office? There's a bed over—"

"It's still my office! I may have allowed you to occupy other areas of the factory. But no one, and I mean no one, will be moving into my office." He hobbled across the floor, and gazed out of the window.

"There's one thing I've never really understood, Tobias."

"What now?"

"After you'd lost your leg, how — err — where — err — did you come by *that*?" He pointed to Socky's wooden leg.

"You mean Albert." Socky tapped it.

"Albert?"

"That's what I call him. I got him from Limbs-A-Plenty. It's a thriving little business in Ghost Town. When I came around, and discovered that I was — err — "

"Dead?"

"A ghost. I took one step, and then fell over. That's when I realised that my leg had gone. Very inconvenient."

"I can see how it would be."

"Someone suggested I go to Limbs-A-Plenty. They had a number of different colours available, but I thought the natural wood look was best. Don't you agree?"

"Definitely. Anyway, I was just thinking that you'd be much more at home living somewhere like the museum. They have lots of old things there."

"*Old things*? What makes you think I have anything in common with *old things*?"

"There'd be other ghosts from your era there. You'd have something to talk about — like socks and stuff."

"I'm sorry, young man, but that simply isn't going to happen. This is my office, and I plan to stay here."

"Well, I'm sorry too, Tobias, but another flatmate will be moving in here very soon."

"Over my dead body."

"Quite likely."

Neil could see he wasn't going to change Socky's mind, so he re-joined the others.

"Well?" Dorothy said.

"No chance. Tobias Fotheringham is not for moving."

"Sometimes I wonder if it's worth it." Charlie picked up a bottle of eye drops, leaned his head back and put a couple of drops into each eye. "I like it here in Washbridge, among the humans, but life was so much easier back in Candlefield. At least we could be ourselves there."

"Yeah, but there's no internet in Candlefield." Neil grabbed his iPad. "No Facebook, no Twitter, no videos of a pig wearing a funny hat."

"I don't get it." Charlie had his eyes shut tight as the eye drops kicked in. "We're meant to be *super*natural. How come we can't get online in Candlefield? If humans can do it, surely we can?"

"We could if it wasn't for the Combined Sup Council," Dorothy said. "They're stuck in their ways. They block the idea every time it's floated."

"Looks like we're stuck here in Washbridge, then." Neil tapped his watch. "Have you seen the time? It's a quarter to nine. We'd better get a move on."

Just then, there was a knock on the door.

"Don't answer it," Neil said, in little more than a whisper. "It'll be Redman."

"How do you know?" Dorothy spoke in the same hushed tone.

"Who else would it be? He knows he'll catch us in at this time of day."

A second knock—louder this time. "I know you're in there!"

"Told you." Neil looked at the other two.

"We may as well answer it." Charlie shrugged his

enormous shoulders. "He isn't going to go away."

"But we don't have his money," Dorothy said.

He knocked a third time—even louder.

Charlie unlocked the door. "Morning, Mr Redman. We were just on our way out."

"Think again." Redman was a bruiser of a werewolf who towered over even Charlie. The rumour was he'd once been big in Mixed Martial Arts. "You three and I are going to have a little chat."

"Couldn't we do it tonight, Mr Redman?" Neil's voice betrayed his nervousness.

"We either do it now, or you'll find the locks have been changed when you get home tonight."

"Legally, I don't think you can do that," Neil said.

The other two looked at him as though he'd lost his mind. Redman took two steps forward, and stooped down so his face was inches from Neil's. "Sorry, little wizard boy. What did you just say?"

"Of course, I could be wrong," Neil conceded.

"Sit over there!" Redman pointed to the sofa in front of the picture window.

Although it was a three-seater, Charlie took up almost two seats, so Neil was forced to perch on the arm.

"Mr Redman, I know we're late with—"

"Did I ask you to speak?" Redman fixed Neil with his gaze.

"No. Sorry."

"You're late with the rent—*again!*"

"Ten days isn't all that late." Dorothy hoped her smile might win him over.

"You're ten days late on this month's rent, but over forty days late on last month's."

"Last month's?" Dorothy and Charlie both glared at Neil.

"I can explain, guys."

"Not on my time you can't," Redman continued. "You three can sort out your little squabbles in your own time. Right now, you're going to listen to me. It's obvious to anyone with even half a brain, which presumably rules out you three, that you're never going to make rent until you get someone in the fourth bedroom."

"We've been trying," Charlie said.

"Not hard enough. It's over three months since we last had this same conversation, and you still haven't found anyone. So, now it's my turn."

"What do you mean?" Dorothy looked worried. "Your turn?"

"You three are never going to find someone to take the fourth room, so I'm going to find someone for you."

"Hold on!" Neil stood up, but then immediately thought better of it, and sat back down again. "That isn't on. We should be the ones to decide who lives with us."

"Oh, I'm so sorry. Am I being unfair? Do all of you feel that way?"

"Yeah." Charlie nodded.

Dorothy nodded too.

"How very thoughtless of me. There is one other option." Redman hesitated. "The three of you can pack your stuff, and be out of here by five o'clock tonight. Now, which is it to be?"

"I guess it wouldn't be so bad if you found someone," Charlie said.

"Yeah, that would be okay." Neil managed a weak smile.

"I'm cool with that." Dorothy agreed.

"Cool! Then we're all agreed." Redman started for the door. "You can expect your new flatmate within the next few days. Make them welcome."

"Did you have someone in mind?" Neil called after him.

"Someone who is tidier than you three." Redman glanced around the room. "That shouldn't be difficult." He slammed the door behind him.

"I can explain, guys!" Neil said, when the other two turned on him.

"This had better be good." Charlie looked ready to tear his flatmate's head off.

"You remember when I told you that my car had blown a head gasket last month."

"Yeah?"

"I used the rent to pay for the repair."

"Not cool, dude," Charlie said. "You should have told us."

"I thought I'd be able to pay it back without you two having to know."

"You should have said something, Neil," Dorothy said. "We'd have understood."

"I know, and I'm sorry."

"Looks like we're going to get a new flatmate sooner than we thought, Socky or no Socky."

Neil started towards the door.

"You two go on ahead," Charlie said. "I've just remembered something."

"What now?" Neil sighed.

"I've got an ingrown toe nail. I need to cut it, or I'll be hobbling around all day."

Once Charlie was sure the other two had left the

building, he went onto the landing and called, "Pretty. Come on, Pretty! Hurry up or you'll miss your morning milk. Pretty! Pretty!"

He hadn't noticed the young, brunette witch coming down the stairs from the floor above.

"Pretty!"

"Why thank you, kind sir."

He blushed. "Sorry, I didn't mean you—err—that's to say, you are pretty, but I—err—was calling—err."

She flashed him a sexy smile, and carried on down the stairs.

"Oh boy!" He wanted the floor to open up and swallow him.

Just then, a ginger cat came running up the stairs, and began to rub against Charlie's legs.

"Where have you been, Pretty? I've just made a complete fool of myself because of you. Come on, we'll have to be quick this morning, or I'll be late for work."

The cat followed him into the apartment where it obviously knew its way to the kitchen. It weaved around Charlie's legs while he took the milk from the fridge, and poured it into a saucer. "There you go, girl. Drink up."

The cat was lapping the milk even before Charlie had let go of the saucer.

"Don't make a mess. If the others find out I've let you in again, they'll kill me."

Within less than a minute, the cat had licked the saucer dry, and began to meow.

"Sorry, I haven't got any food. I'll bring some home for you tonight."

He picked up the saucer, rinsed it under the tap, then grabbed the cat, and hurried downstairs and out of the door. "See you tonight, Pretty."

"Did you buy that lame story about the ingrown toenail?" Dorothy said, as Neil drove them into town.

"Why? Do you think he was lying?"

"Of course he was. I bet you this month's rent that he's been feeding that stupid cat again."

"You don't know that for sure."

"I'll know when we get back tonight. I marked the milk bottle this morning when I was putting my blood back into the fridge."

Neil laughed. "You marked the milk bottle?"

"Of course I did. I know what he's like. As soon as our backs are turned, he lets that smelly cat into the apartment. You know the terms of the lease: no animals other than caged birds are allowed. We're already in Redman's bad books. If Charlie gets us thrown out because of a stupid cat, I'll swing for him."

"I hope Redman gets us a pretty young witch."

"Don't you have enough women on the go at the moment?"

"I can't help it if all women find me irresistible."

"Not *all* women."

"Okay, but you're the exception, and I still think you're playing hard to get."

Chapter 3

"What are you doing down here, Carly?" Dougal shouted. "Are you lost?"

Carly blushed, but didn't respond to his jibe.

"Over here, Carly." Susan stood up and waved to her.

"I don't know how you can work with these pigs," Carly said when she reached Susan's desk.

"I've dealt with worse."

"I've just taken an ad which might interest you. I called your extension, but it was engaged."

"Sorry, I've been on the phone most of the morning."

"It's a flat-share, and it looks pretty good to me." She dropped the copy on Susan's desk. "You'll have to move quickly though because I reckon it'll get snapped up."

"Four-way share? I'd hoped to find a two-way. Still, it does look good."

"It is. Those loft-style apartments are quite new, and from what I hear, they're enormous. They're in what used to be the old sock factory."

"Thanks, Carly. I owe you one."

"No problem. Stella told me what you did to Bob Bragg. He's had that coming for ages. Good luck with the apartment."

***

"What?" The man shouted so loudly that Susan had to move the phone away from her ear.

"I said I'm calling about the flat-share."

"How do you know about it already? The ad isn't in the paper until tomorrow. If you're a friend of those three losers, you can forget it."

"I work at The Bugle. The people in ad sales alerted me to your ad."

"Oh, okay. Do you want to see it?"

"That would be great. When?"

"It'll have to be this afternoon—two o'clock. It's the only time I can make it, today."

"I'm at work."

"Please yourself, but the first person to see it will take it."

"Okay. I'll be there. Will the other tenants want to interview me too?"

"Other—? Oh, wait, do you think I'm one of the tenants?"

"That's what I'd assumed."

"I own the property. Don't worry about the tenants—I'm the one who'll decide if you get the apartment or not. You've got the address, I take it?"

"Yes."

"Be there at two. And don't be late. I hate to be kept waiting."

"Okay, Mr—?"

"Redman."

He'd hung up before Susan could ask him anything else. She thought it a bit weird that the other tenants weren't going to be involved in the process, but anything to get out of that awful motel.

***

When lunchtime came around, Dougal tried once again to persuade her to join him and his friends in the Walrus and Hammer. She declined. Susan couldn't imagine anything worse than spending an hour in their company, watching them get hammered. Instead, she ate an egg and cress sandwich at her desk. She'd bought it on the way into work that morning.

"You can't stay in here all lunch hour, Susan," Stella said.

"I'm okay. I've had a sandwich."

"Why don't you come and have a coffee with me?"

"Okay. I suppose it would do me good to stretch my legs."

"Have you been in Washbridge long?"

"Only a few days. I've lived in London for the last five years."

"You'll notice a difference, then. The pace of life up here is much slower."

"I know. I was actually born here."

"Really? When did you leave?"

"When I went to uni. After I'd got my degree, I found a job in London, and I've lived there ever since."

"Do you still have family up here?"

"Yes. All my family are still in Washbridge."

"They'll be pleased to have you back."

Susan nodded. She wasn't about to tell Stella that none of her family knew she was back.

"I thought we'd try the coffee shop just down the road. It's a bit unusual, but as you've been living in London, it'll probably seem quite tame to you. It's called Coffee Triangle."

"Strange name."

"You'll see why when we get inside."

There weren't any triangles to be seen, but there were

plenty of tambourines. Almost everybody in the shop was holding one.

"What's this all about?" Susan asked Stella when they'd taken their seats.

"It's a percussion themed shop."

"Well, London or not, this is a first for me."

"Every day of the week, they feature a different percussion instrument. There's drum day, gong day and triangle day. Everyone is given one of the featured instruments to play while they drink their coffee."

"It must get awfully noisy in here on drum day and gong day."

"It's terrible. I always avoid those days. I've got us a couple of tambourines if you'd like to have a go."

"No, I'm okay. You go ahead."

"Stella gave her tambourine a quick shake. "What on earth made you decide to come back to this dead end place?"

"I needed a job. I've worked at a couple of newspapers in London. The last one folded three months after I joined."

"That was bad luck."

"I heard about this position through a friend, and thought I'd give it a shot. Besides which, I was ready for a new challenge."

"Well, you'll certainly get that here. I assume you've heard of The Bugle's reputation?"

"Yeah, but Fred Flynn seems determined to change it."

"He's going to have his work cut out with that bunch of no-hopers in the newsroom. Present company excepted, of course. I'd been looking for another job for quite some time, but then when The Bugle was sold, I thought maybe things would change for the better, so I decided to hang around a little longer." She took a sip of coffee. "Where are you living, Susan?"

"I'm staying in a motel on the outskirts of Washbridge. It's called The Luxury, which is an absolute joke because it's a flea pit. The shower is next to useless. I can't wait to get out of there."

"Can't you stay with family?"

"I'd rather not. Anyway, fingers crossed, I might have found somewhere. I talked to Carly in classified ads, and she's put me onto an ad that's going to be in tomorrow morning's paper. It's a four-way flat-share in a loft-style apartment a few miles out of the town centre."

"That sounds promising."

"I'm going to see it later today, so fingers crossed."

***

"Flynn, do you have a moment?" Susan popped her head around his door.

"Sure, come on in."

"Look, I realise this is my first day, but is there any chance I can take some time off this afternoon? I'm living in a motel at the moment, but I have the chance of a flat-share. The only time I can see—"

"Stop!" He put up his hand. "I don't expect you to clock in and out. The only thing I expect from you is results. I need big stories. Stories that are going to turn this newspaper around."

"Okay. That's great. Thanks very much."

Susan was just about to climb into her car when her phone rang. Caller ID told her it was Caroline Day, or

Dreams as Susan still knew her. They'd known each other since they were kids—Caroline had always been hair brained—away with the fairies. That's how she'd got the nickname Daydreams, which had been shortened to Dreams.

"Hey, Dreams. How's it going?"

"Okay. Are you in Washbridge, yet?"

"Yeah, I started the new job today. I'm just on my way to look at an apartment."

"Where have you been staying?"

"In a seedy little motel called Luxury, if you can believe it."

"Oh, goodness. I know that place. It's a real dump! Why are you staying there?"

"It was all I could get at short notice. Besides, I didn't want to blow a fortune staying in the town centre."

"What about your mum? Does she know you're back?"

"Not yet, I'll tell her once I've got somewhere to live."

"How is she?"

"Mum's fine."

"Are you and your dad still not speaking?"

"No. It's been nearly two years now."

"Have you told your mum about the new job?"

"No. You're the only person who knows."

"Where's this apartment you're going to look at?"

"On Colbourn Drive."

"I know the ones. From all accounts, they're very nice, but they must be expensive. Can you afford it?"

"It's a four-way share. It's the only thing I've even had a sniff of so far. Anyway, I'd better go because I've got to be there at two. The landlord sounds a nasty piece of work. I reckon if I'm even a minute late, he'll have left. Catch you later, Dreams."

Susan was struggling to find a parking space, but then someone pulled out as she was doing her second circuit of the road. It wasn't the best bit of parking she'd ever done, but it would have to do. Susan checked her watch; it was five to two. She'd have to run.

The apartment was on the middle floor of five. A giant of a man was waiting for her.

"Are you Susan Hall?" he growled.

"Yeah." She was still trying to catch her breath.

"You only just made it. I thought you'd changed your mind."

"No. I'm still interested."

"Okay, but I've only got about thirty minutes, so you'll have to look sharp."

"No problem. Thanks."

He took out a set of keys from his pocket, and unlocked the door.

"Aren't any of the other tenants in?"

"No. Like I said before, it's only me you have to worry about. If I'm happy with you, and you want the place, then that's all that matters. The others can like it or lump it."

Susan didn't like the sound of that.

"You can see for yourself that it's a big apartment. There's a nice view over the river. This place cost me a fortune, and look at the state of it. Those three wasters don't know the meaning of the word 'tidy'."

Susan couldn't argue with that. The apartment was tastefully decorated, and the furniture looked expensive. But there was stuff everywhere, and the sink was full of dishes. These were not the sort of people Susan would normally have chosen to live with. But what choice did she have?

"That would be your room, over there." He pointed. "Take a look."

The bedroom was way tidier than the rest of the apartment. It was also much colder. And very spacious — it was easily three times the size of the bedroom she'd had in London, but then renting in the capital came at a premium. She couldn't fault the apartment. It was big, it was modern, and it was close enough to where she worked. The only nagging doubts in her mind were the temperature in the bedroom, and the other flatmates. If they'd been there, she could have made a judgment as to whether she'd be able to live with them or not. But she was going to have to make that decision blind.

"What do you think?" He checked his watch. "Do you want it or not?"

"It's very cold in this room."

"That's because no one's lived in it for a while. It will soon warm up."

"Do you need to know right now?"

"That's up to you. But it's first come, first served."

"Okay, yeah. I'll take it."

"I'll need one month's rent in advance, plus five hundred pounds as security."

"Is a cheque okay?"

"Yes, but if it bounces, I'll be forced to rip your throat out." He laughed.

Chapter 4

"Charlie, can you help me, please?"

He turned around. It was Ali, a pretty young witch, who came to the gym most days. She was on one of the treadmills, gesturing for him to come over.

"Hi, Ali. You're becoming a regular visitor."

"Gotta keep fit, Charlie. Look, I know I'm a bit ditzy, but I can't remember how to change the settings. Do you think you could show me?"

"Did you swipe your membership card?"

"Yeah, I've done that already."

"In that case, all you need to do is press the Start button, and it will remember the settings from the last time you used it."

"Is that all? Silly me. Thanks, Charlie." She pressed the button, and began to jog slowly on the machine.

He walked back across the room to join Mason, one of the other instructors. Like Charlie, he was a werewolf.

"You do realise that Ali has the hots for you, don't you?" Mason said while taking a sip from his power drink.

"Don't be stupid. She just needed help with the treadmill."

"Of course she didn't. How many times has she asked you to help her with that same treadmill?"

"Most days. I guess she's not very technically minded."

"Really? Charlie, you're a total chump. How technically minded does she need to be to press the Start button? It's any excuse to get you to go over and talk to her. Don't you realise that you and me are the reason a lot of these women come in here?"

"You're just vain, Mason." Charlie shook his head. "They come here to keep fit."

"Some of them do, sure, but how do you think I pull so many women? I just give them a smile, and ask for their number."

"I'm not like you."

"You could be. You've got everything going for you. You're a fit young guy, and not totally unattractive."

"Gee, thanks."

"All you have to do is flash them a smile, and give them the chat. That's it. Why don't you go over there, and ask Ali if she'd like to go out for a drink tonight?"

"The chat?"

"Yeah. Just turn on the charm. They love that."

"I wouldn't know where to start."

"I'll show you, if you like. Why don't I ask Ali if she'd like to go for a drink with you?"

"Don't you dare! I'll kill you if you say anything. Anyway, there's someone else I've got my eye on."

"Who's that?"

"A witch who lives in the same apartment block as me. I see her sometimes in the mornings. She's gorgeous."

"Have you spoken to her?"

"Not exactly. Although she did think I'd called her pretty."

"Think? Were you mumbling again?"

"No. I was calling the cat. Her name is Pretty."

"You have a cat?"

"It's not mine. I don't know whose it is. It comes to our apartment to be fed."

"You're a real soft touch, aren't you, Charlie. So what happened with you and the gorgeous witch?"

"Nothing, really. Like I said, I was calling the cat when the witch walked by. She said, *'Oh, thank you, kind sir'*."

"That was your opportunity. What did you say? Did you ask her out?"

"No, I just said, *'Sorry, I was talking to the cat'*."

"You're hopeless! Why don't I come over to your place? I could put a word in for you."

"No. I know what you're like. You'd only embarrass me, and make things ten times worse."

"I'd quite like to come over sometime, anyway. I've still got a thing for Dorothy."

"You're wasting your time there. She's sworn off men."

"That's what they all say, but then they meet me."

"You're so full of yourself, Mason."

"That's the whole point. You've got to have self-confidence. That's what attracts the ladies. Anyway, what did you get up to on the FM?"

"Just the usual. I went to the Range in Candlefield, and let loose in there. It was busier than usual — really packed. What about you?"

"I didn't go back to Candlefield, that's for sure. Where's the fun in that? What's the point of being a werewolf if every full moon you hide away in Candlefield? It's much more exciting to stay here and scare a few humans."

"I hope you didn't hurt anyone."

"Of course not. I'm not stupid. I don't want the Rogue Retrievers on my back. I just howled a little, bared my teeth, and generally scared a few humans. Nothing I could get arrested for."

Just then, Ali came walking across the room. "Charlie, do you think you could give me a hand with the cross-trainer?"

Mason winked at him.

***

It was Charlie's early finish. On the way back home, he stopped off at the local supermarket to pick up some tins of cat food. He couldn't bring himself to give Pretty the budget brand, so instead bought the top of the range. When he got back to the apartment, Pretty was waiting outside the door.

"You're going to get me in trouble," he said quietly, in case anyone overheard. "The others don't want you here."

The cat just meowed and circled his legs.

"Come on then, quickly." Charlie went into the kitchen, found the can opener, and opened the deluxe salmon mix. As soon as he'd put the bowl down on the floor, the cat was straight on it.

Charlie put the empty tin at the bottom of the bin, then hid the other three at the back of the cupboard that contained all the cleaning materials. He didn't want Dorothy to see them because she hated the cat with a passion. He knew he shouldn't encourage Pretty, but he couldn't bring himself to ignore her. She was such a sweet little thing.

He left the cat eating her food, and went through to his bedroom.

"Hey, Charlie!" A tiny voice came from the other side of the room. "Come over here."

He peered through the large magnifying glass which was on the cupboard. "Hey there, you two. How are you?"

Charlie had been touched when he'd heard about the plight of the starlight fairies. A number of them were homeless, but even more of them wanted to move to the human world. Being so tiny, they were unable to do so by themselves. They could only make the move if they could find a sponsor. Being the big-hearted guy he was, he had put his name forward. Most sponsors took only one starlight fairy through to the human world, but he had agreed to take two.

The two fairies: one named Greta, the other Bunty, had been friends since childhood, and didn't want to be split up. Transporting them to Washbridge had been a delicate operation. Starlight fairies were the size of a pinhead, and made their homes inside specially designed thimbles. One wrong move and the houses could have been destroyed, and the starlight fairies killed. But he'd made it, and the two fairies now lived on top of the cupboard in his bedroom. The initial plan had been that they would stay with him on a temporary basis, perhaps a few months. They'd been there for two years now, and seemed in no hurry to move out. Their reluctance to move might have had something to do with the fact that Charlie didn't have the heart to charge them rent.

As the fairies were so small, the only way that he could see them properly was to look through the large magnifying glass that he'd set up in front of the thimbles. In order to hear what they said, he'd also placed a small microphone next to the thimble houses.

He had a very good relationship with both of the fairies, even though they were very different in character. Greta was similar in nature to Charlie. She was easy-going, caring, and good-natured. Bunty was an entirely different proposition. She could be brash, and quite cruel with her words sometimes. He felt sorry for Greta when Bunty turned on her. Fortunately, most of the time they got on well together.

He always left the window of his bedroom slightly ajar so the two fairies could come and go as they pleased. They spent a lot of their time outdoors. He would also occasionally leave the door to his bedroom open. That way the fairies could have the run of the apartment. Neil and Dorothy knew that the fairies were in Charlie's room. They'd seen the thimbles, the magnifying glass and the microphone. What they didn't know was that the fairies spent a lot of time flying around the rest of the apartment. Although it had never been Charlie's intention, the two fairies had become his eyes and ears.

"I like your new girlfriend, Charlie," Greta said. Bunty was by her side.

"What new girlfriend?" He looked puzzled.

"The brunette witch from the floor above."

Charlie blushed. "She's not my girlfriend."

"Are you sure? She seems to be very fond of you."

"I've barely spoken to her."

"You said she was pretty."

"You heard that?" He blushed even deeper. "That was just a mistake. I was calling the cat."

"Don't you think it's rather a coincidence the way she keeps bumping into you?" Greta said.

"We're just neighbours."

"And you're never likely to be more than that unless you make a move," Bunty said. "What's the matter with you, man? Why don't you give her a kiss?"

"Don't be stupid. I barely know her."

"Didn't you see the look on her face? And hear the way she spoke to you? She's fallen for you, Charlie, but you're just too blind to see it."

"I'm sure you're mistaken."

"You're always the same, Charlie." Bunty shook her head. "You're absolutely hopeless when it comes to women. You can't read them at all, can you?"

"Leave him alone, Bunty," Greta said. "Everyone does things in their own time, and in their own way."

"And how long do you think she's going to wait around for Charlie to make a move? She's very pretty. There'll be other suitors interested in her. He needs to get off his backside, and ask her out for a drink. Why don't you, Charlie?"

"I could never do that."

"See?" Bunty turned to Greta. "What did I tell you? He's hopeless."

Just then, Charlie heard a noise coming from somewhere inside the apartment. It couldn't be Neil or Dorothy; they didn't finish work until much later. He crept out of his bedroom, and listened. Another noise. It seemed to come from the fourth bedroom. Had somebody broken in? If so, they were going to regret it.

He edged across the room, and gently pushed open the door of the vacant bedroom. He was all set to go werewolf on the intruder when a woman turned around, obviously shocked to see him.

"You made me jump!" she said.

Charlie let the werewolf go back inside. "Who are you?"

"Susan Hall. I'm your new flatmate."

"Oh? I had no idea we had one."

"The landlord, Mr Redman, said I could move in straight away."

"I didn't even realise he'd shown anyone the apartment."

"I only viewed it an hour ago. I did ask him if I could meet the other tenants before making a decision, but he said I had to decide there and then. I'm sorry about this. I know it's not the way things are usually done."

"It's not your fault."

"I really like the place. There's just one thing: it's really cold in this room. Is it always like this?"

Charlie couldn't see Socky—he was only visible to Neil and the fairies—but he could sense when he was around. Charlie knew that the temperature had more to do with that ghostly presence than the heating system.

"I'm sure it will warm up once you've moved in. Do you live in Washbridge?"

"I've been living in London for the last five years, but I've just got a job up here. I've been staying in a motel a few miles outside of Washbridge. It's a real flea-pit, so I'm really looking forward to moving in here."

"Sorry, I didn't introduce myself. I'm Charlie. I work at a gym in the town centre. It's my early finish today."

Just then, the bedroom door slid open and Pretty walked in, meowing loudly.

"We have a cat?"

"No. And, you haven't seen her. Okay?"

Susan looked puzzled.

"We're not allowed to keep pets in the apartment, but Pretty—"

"Pretty?"

"Yeah, that's what it says on her name tag. She comes around most days, and I feed her. Do me a favour, don't tell the others, will you? Neil's not too bothered, but Dorothy hates cats. If she knew I was feeding her, she'd go mad."

"Dorothy and Neil? Are they the two other flatmates?"

"Yeah. The three of us all used to work together at a fancy dress shop. Neil still works there. Dorothy now works in a bookshop."

"You all used to live *and* work together? Wasn't that a bit much?"

"It was. What about you? What do you do?"

"I'm an investigative reporter; I started work at The Bugle today. I heard about the job through a friend."

"Do you know people in Washbridge, then?"

"Yeah, I'm from here originally. I've still got friends in the area, and family."

"Investigative reporter, eh? Sounds exciting."

"It can be, but it's also very challenging. The Bugle's hoping to change its image, but to do that they need to break big stories. It's my job to bring them in." Susan led the way out of the bedroom. "Why don't I make us a cup of tea?"

"That'd be nice. If you can find any clean cups. We're a bit behind with the washing up."

"So I see."

It took a while, but Susan eventually managed to find a couple of clean mugs in the cupboard. "What's that?" She pointed to the two bottles of synthetic blood on the middle shelf of the fridge.

"That? Err — that belongs to Dorothy."

"What is it?" Susan picked one of them up. "It looks

horrible!"

"It's some sort of iron supplement that Dorothy has to take."

She sniffed at the milk; it seemed to be okay. "Why did the landlord decide to take it upon himself to find you a new flatmate?" Susan had been curious about that ever since Redman had told her that he wasn't going to consult the other tenants.

"It's our own fault." Charlie took a slurp of tea. "We've been behind on the rent for a while now. The three of us barely make enough to cover it. Split four ways, it should be more manageable. We've been looking for someone for a while, but we've never been able to find anyone suitable."

"How long have you been trying?"

"It must be three months, probably more. Anyway, Redman got fed up of waiting, and said he was going to find someone."

"Do you think the others are going to be okay with me moving in?"

"Yeah, I'm sure they will."

"I suppose I'd better get off," Susan said when she'd finished her tea. "I'm going to the motel to get my stuff. What time will the others be back?"

"Difficult to say. Usually before six."

"I'm not sure if I'll be back by then. Tell them I look forward to meeting them, will you?

"Okay, see you later, Susan."

Charlie took a deep breath. Holy moly! Their new flatmate was a human. That was going to be awkward. They'd never had to worry about hiding the fact that they were sups, but that was all going to change, particularly for Neil, who routinely used magic around the apartment. He was going to have to tone that down pretty quickly or they'd all be in trouble. Not only was she a human, she was also an investigative reporter who was looking to break big stories, and what bigger story than the presence of supernatural creatures in Washbridge?

This wasn't good.

Chapter 5

Neil spotted the two young women as soon as they walked into his shop. They were both very pretty, but he was particularly taken with the blonde who had a cheeky smile. His assistant, a witch named Debs, was attending to the only other customer in the shop, so Neil made his way over to the young women, who were in the costume section.

"Hi there, you two. Anything I can help you beautiful ladies with?"

The one with the cheeky smile blushed. "We're going to a fancy dress party."

"Well, you're in the right shop."

"Oh, yeah." She giggled. "I suppose we are."

"What were you thinking of going as?"

"Judy has picked out a witch costume. I thought I'd go as a fairy."

"We have lots of fairy costumes. Have you seen them?"

"Yeah. The thing is, I was hoping to go as a green fairy."

"Green? That's a little unusual."

"You only seem to have white, pink or yellow fairy costumes."

"I'm sure there must be a green one in there somewhere." Neil ushered them to one side. Then, with his back to them, he picked up one of the pink fairy costumes, and cast a spell to turn it green.

"Look, here's one. Is that the sort of thing you're looking for?"

The two women looked astonished, as well they might. They'd been through the rack three times, and there had been no sign of a green fairy costume.

"Yeah? That looks great."

"Is there anything else I can help you with?"

"No, thanks. We'll just take these two costumes."

Neil put them into a bag, and took the payment. "Here you are." He gave the blonde his business card. "If you need anything else, anything at all, just give me a call on that number." He flashed her a smile, and she blushed again.

After they'd left, Neil turned around to find Debs standing behind him. She was giving him 'that' look of hers.

"What's up with you?" he said.

"You're dicing with death, Neil."

"What do you mean? I was only being friendly to the customers."

"I don't mean your outrageous flirting. I saw what you did with that fairy costume. You changed it from pink to green."

"They didn't see me do it."

"They'd already been through the rack. They knew there weren't any green ones, and yet somehow you managed to produce one out of thin air. Don't you think they might have found that a bit suspicious?"

"You worry too much, Debs. You should loosen up. Why don't you come for a drink with me tonight? That'll cheer you up."

"I don't need cheering up. I told you when you interviewed me for this job that I don't mix work and pleasure. If Johnny knew you were trying to chat me up, he'd come around here and sort you out."

"I'm not trying to chat you up. I'm just being friendly. What do you see in Johnny, anyway?"

"He's a real man. That's what I see in him."

"He's not a man at all. He's a werewolf. He's all muscles and no brains."

"Watch it! If I tell him what you've said, he'll rip your head off."

Just then, two customers walked into the shop, and Debs hurried over to assist them.

Neil had badly misjudged Debs. When Charlie and Dorothy had resigned and left him in the lurch, he'd decided that he was going to employ some pretty young things, but Debs had turned out to be a nightmare. She was totally impervious to his charms.

Two kids came into the shop, and began to mess around in the far corner. They'd been in lots of times before, and never bought anything. They usually played with the stock, and then left it scattered around for Neil to tidy up. He wasn't going to stand for it today. Neil checked to make sure that Debs wasn't watching—he didn't need another ear-bashing from her. When he was sure she was occupied, he cast a spell that made the mask, which the kids were playing with, start to talk. They dropped it and rushed, screaming, out of the shop.

After work, Neil called in at the bookshop where Dorothy worked, to see if she wanted a lift.

"No, thanks. I'm going to stay a little longer. Molly said she'll give me a lift home."

"Okay, see you back at the apartment."

As Neil made his way to his car, he thanked his lucky stars that neither Charlie nor Dorothy knew anything about cars. They'd fallen for his story about having to spend last month's rent on the cylinder head gasket. He'd actually spent the money on a new watch. Both Charlie and Dorothy had seen it, but he'd told them it was a present from his grandmother. He was way too smart for those two.

***

Back at the apartment, the first thing Neil saw when he walked in was the cat.

"Charlie, you'd better get rid of that thing. Dorothy will be home soon. She's getting a lift with Molly. If it's still here when she gets back, she'll chuck it out of the window, and you after it, most likely."

"Okay." Charlie gathered up Pretty in his arms, and put her out of the door. "There you go, Pretty." He'd no sooner said the words than the witch, who he'd bumped into earlier that day, came walking up the stairs.

"Are you doing this on purpose?" She flashed him another sexy smile. "Pretending to see to the cat just so you can bump into me?"

"No!" Charlie blushed. "I was just—err—I was putting Pretty out." He tapped the cat on the backside. "Go on, Pretty. Go away before Dorothy comes home."

"Dorothy? Oh, I'm sorry, I didn't realise you had a girlfriend." She sounded disappointed.

"Dorothy isn't my girlfriend. We're just flatmates. There are three of us. Well, four now, I guess."

"That's okay then." She smiled and carried on upstairs.

Neil had been listening at the open door.

"What's wrong with you, Charlie?"

"What do you mean?"

"Can't you see that she fancies you?"

"Who?"

"Who do you think? The brunette you've just been talking to on the stairs."

"Don't be daft. I just happened to bump into her."

"She fancies you something rotten."

"You're wrong."

"Charlie, you're hopeless. Look, why don't I put a word in for you?"

"No, don't you dare! Anyway, never mind about that. You'll never guess what. We've got a new flatmate."

"Where are they?"

"*She* was here earlier."

"She?" Neil beamed.

"Yeah, but there's bad news."

"Don't tell me she's old and ugly."

"No. It's not that." Charlie hesitated.

"What then?"

"She's a human."

"A human, eh? Is she a looker?"

"Yeah. She's pretty, and she seems really smart."

"Everybody seems smart to you, Charlie."

"Watch it!"

"I'm glad she's a human," Neil said. "The last thing we needed was another ice maiden vampire, like Dorothy. So what's her name, this human?"

"Susan. I can't remember her last name."

"And where is she now?"

"Gone to get her stuff from the motel. She should be back soon, but there's something else you need to know about her."

"Don't tell me she's got a boyfriend."

"She works at The Bugle."

"That rag? What does she do? Sell ads? Or is she a

secretary?"

"No, she's a reporter. An investigative reporter."

"Interesting."

"No, not interesting. It's bad — very bad. You do know what an investigative reporter does, don't you?"

"Let me think about it." Neil scratched his chin. "Do they investigate stuff?"

"They're on the lookout for big stories."

"So?"

"Don't you think that the presence of supernatural creatures here in Washbridge might constitute a big story?"

"Yeah, but she's never going to find out, is she?"

"She will if you don't curb your magic."

"I don't use it that much."

"Yes, you do. You don't even realise you're doing it half the time. You won't be able to once she's moved in."

"It'll be fine. Don't worry. I think I'll take a shower and get changed. I want to give a good first impression to this new flatmate of ours."

Charlie rolled his eyes. He might have known that would be Neil's reaction. All he could think about was whether he could pull their new flatmate.

The sink was still full of dishes, so Charlie decided he'd better wash them because no one else was going to. He'd no sooner started than the door opened, and Susan walked in. She was struggling to carry three suitcases.

Charlie quickly wiped his hands, and rushed over. "Here, let me take those."

"I'm okay," she said, but she clearly wasn't.

He grabbed the three cases, and took them through to her room. When he came back out, Susan had picked up the tea towel.

"You don't need to do that," he said. "This is our mess. We should clear it up."

"We're flatmates now, aren't we? You wash. I'll wipe."

They were still at it when Neil reappeared. He was bare-chested, wearing only jeans.

"Oh?" he said, rubbing his hair with a towel. "I didn't realise we had company."

Charlie glared at him. He knew full well that Neil must have heard Susan come in. This was typical of him. "Neil, this is Susan, our new flatmate."

"Hi. Pleased to meet you." Neil walked over to the kitchen. We've been looking for a new flatmate for ages. You'll fit the bill nicely."

She offered her hand, but instead of shaking it, he put it to his lips, and kissed it gently. If he thought that would impress her, he was sadly wrong.

"Charlie tells me you work at The Bugle."

"Yeah, I started there today."

"An investigative reporter, eh?"

"That's right."

"Sounds exciting. Where did you work before?"

"In London."

"Why would you leave there for this backwater?"

"I actually grew up in Washbridge. I left when I went to uni."

"Do you have family up here?"

"Yeah."

"And friends?"

"A few."

"What about your boyfriend? Is he still in London?"

Susan had met men like Neil before.

Or at least that's what she thought.

Chapter 6

"Why do you always act so cold towards him?" Molly asked, after Dorothy had refused Neil's offer of a lift home. Molly was a fellow vampire who had started work at the bookshop six months before Dorothy.

"He gets on my nerves, and he's always trying to hit on me. I wish I could afford my own car so I wouldn't have to rely on him."

"I think he's rather cute." Molly grinned.

"Yeah, but then you think any male with a pulse is cute. Come to think of it, you've even been out with a few that don't have a pulse."

"Hey! You cheeky mare. That's not true. Well, not entirely. Neil's a good-looking guy."

"You're right. He is. The problem is, he knows it. That's why I quit my job at the fancy dress shop. He was doing my head in. It's bad enough sharing an apartment with him, but working with him all day too? No, thank you very much."

"Do you think he might go out with me?"

"Of course he will. Just flutter your eyelashes, and he'll come running."

"Is it okay if I come up to your apartment with you when I take you home?"

"Sure, but you'll live to regret it if you hook up with Neil. He'll two time you. And then he'll dump you."

"He won't dump me." Molly smirked. "I'll make sure of that."

"We'll see. Don't say I didn't warn you. Do you know what he had the audacity to do this morning?"

"What?"

"He only took my synthetic blood out of the fridge, and put it in the bread bin."

Molly laughed. "Why did he put it in there?"

"It's not *where* he put it that matters. It's the fact he moved it at all."

"Why did he?"

"Because your darling Neil said it made him feel queasy when he was eating his porridge."

"I suppose the sight of blood can be a bit off-putting to non-vampires."

"Don't tell me you're sticking up for him?"

"No, I'm just saying that not everybody shares our taste for blood."

Dorothy sighed. "Anyway, we'll be getting a new flatmate soon."

"I thought you'd given up on that? How come it's taken so long to find someone?"

"Because of that stupid ghost that Neil invited in. The room is freezing."

"Have you had many people look around?"

"Yeah, loads. The trouble is half of them were humans, and we definitely don't want a human. The others didn't fancy sharing their room with a ghost."

"What makes you so sure you're going to find someone now?"

"It's been taken out of our hands. The landlord came around this morning because we're behind on the rent again. He said he was going to find somebody for us."

"So you don't know who it's going to be?"

"No idea. Another female in the place would be good. I don't think I could handle another guy in there."

"Charlie's all right though, isn't he?"

"Yeah, Charlie's a big softy. He's got a heart of gold, and he's a good-looking guy. Women go crazy for him, but he's totally oblivious. There's a witch on the floor above ours. She's always flirting outrageously with him, but he doesn't even realise. But much as I like Charlie, he drives me crazy with those stupid fairies and that smelly cat."

"I didn't think you could have pets in your apartment."

"We can't, but Charlie has practically adopted a stray. It turns up once or twice a day. I've warned him that if Redman catches us with a cat in the apartment, we'll all be thrown out. Besides which, I've never liked cats. They all have an attitude problem. I have a friend, Jill, she was the one who got me my first job in Washbridge. She has a cat in her office, and it's the ugliest thing you ever did see. It's only got one eye. She calls it Blinky, or Dinky, or something."

"I didn't realise Charlie still had those two fairies in his room."

"They've become a permanent fixture. I could understand it if he was charging them rent, but he's letting them stay there for free."

"That sounds like Charlie."

"I don't know how he puts up with them. All they do is squabble. And that Bunty? She's a real piece of work."

***

"Are you sure you don't mind if I come up to your apartment?" Molly had that wicked glint in her eye—the one Dorothy had seen many times before.

"I'm telling you, Neil is bad news."

"I'll risk it. And besides, I'm starving. Could you spare a

little of your synthetic blood?"

"Sure, there's a couple of bottles in the fridge. Unless of course, Neil's put them back in the bread bin."

When they got inside, Charlie was sitting at the breakfast bar. Neil was in the lounge, reading a book on his e-reader.

"Hey, gorgeous!" Neil shouted. "Dorothy didn't tell me you were coming. I would have got changed."

"No need." Molly fluttered her eyelashes. "I like that shirt."

Dorothy rolled her eyes.

"Hello, Molly," Charlie shouted.

"Hiya. I hear you've been chatting up your neighbour from upstairs."

"Who told you that?" He blushed. "I've done no such thing."

"No need to be shy, Charlie. Anyway, where's that blood? I'm starving."

Dorothy led the way towards the fridge, and had just pulled the door open, when Charlie slammed it shut again.

"What do you think you're doing?" She glared at him.

"Shush!" He pointed towards the fourth bedroom.

"What's going on?"

"We've got a new flatmate, and she's a—"

"Hi." Susan appeared. "One of you must be Dorothy."

"That's me." Dorothy couldn't believe her eyes. Susan was a human! She turned back to Molly, and realised that her friend's gaze was fixed on Susan's neck. She knew she had to act quickly, so she grabbed Molly by the arm, and dragged her back to the door.

"Have you forgotten you have an appointment in ten

minutes, Molly?"

Molly looked confused. "What appointment?"

Dorothy practically pushed her out of the door.

"She's a human!" Molly said, once they were out on the landing. "Why didn't you tell me?"

"I didn't know. This is the first time I've seen her."

"I'm starving. Can't you just go back in, and get me some synthetic blood?"

"How can I when she's in there?"

"Did you see her neck? I really wanted to sink my teeth into it."

"Time for you to go, Molly." Dorothy ushered her towards the stairs.

After she was sure Molly had left, Dorothy joined the others in the lounge.

"Now we're all together," Susan said. "I'd just like to say that I'm a little embarrassed that I've been dropped on you like this. I realise this isn't the way things are usually done. The landlord offered me the room, and said I had to make a decision right there and then, otherwise I wouldn't get the place."

"Don't worry about it," Charlie said. "It's not your fault. If anything, it's ours for dragging our heels."

"Yeah. Don't worry about it." Neil shuffled along the sofa to get a little closer to Susan. "We're really glad you're here. It's nice to have another female in the place, isn't it, Dorothy?"

"Yeah." Dorothy forced a smile. "Really nice."

"Susan's a reporter," Charlie said.

"For The Bugle?" Dorothy looked horrified.

"Yeah, I started there today."

"She used to work in London," Charlie said. "Didn't you, Susan?"

"That's right."

"Why would you leave London for this dump?" Dorothy clearly thought she was crazy.

"This is my hometown. Anyway, I have to say this apartment is fantastic. It's much larger than I've been used to."

"It needs to be with Charlie around." Neil grinned.

"Shut it, you!" Charlie snapped.

"I tell you what," Susan said. "Why don't I order takeaway for us all, as a thank you for letting me join you? How does pizza sound?"

"I'm up for that," Charlie said.

"Yeah, count me in." Neil gave her a thumbs up.

"Okay." Dorothy couldn't have sounded any less enthusiastic.

Susan brought up an app on her phone, and quickly located a local takeaway.

"I'll just get my credit card, and get it ordered. I won't be long."

As soon as Susan was in her bedroom, Dorothy turned to the other two. "What's going on? We can't have a human living with us!"

"It doesn't look like we have much choice," Neil said. "If Redman has said she can have the room, what are we meant to do about it?"

"I have to get my blood out of the fridge before she sees it." Dorothy stood up.

"She's already seen it," Charlie said. "When she went to get the milk for the tea."

"What did she say?"

"She asked what it was."

"What did you tell her?"

"I said it was an iron supplement that you had to take."

"Did she buy that?"

"She seemed to."

"I've still got to get it out of here." Dorothy hurried over to the fridge, grabbed the two bottles of synthetic blood, and then dashed out of the apartment. After racing up to the next floor, she knocked on the door of the second apartment on the left.

"Dorothy?" A female vampire answered the door. "Are you okay?"

"No, Tilly. I am most decidedly not okay."

"Why? And what's with the blood?"

"I need you to do me a favour."

"Go on."

"Our landlord's let the fourth bedroom to a human."

"He's done what?"

"I know. A human living with us three? How's that ever going to work?"

"It's going to spoil things around here." Tilly sighed. "This whole apartment block has always been human-free. I thought we were going to keep it that way."

"So did I, but we didn't have any say in the matter. Redman's told her she can have the room. I can't keep this blood in the fridge now she's there. Is there any chance you could keep it in yours?"

"No problem. You've got a key to my place, haven't you?"

"Yeah."

"Well then, you can bring it up here and collect it whenever you want."

"Thanks, Tilly. Here." She passed the bottles to her friend. "I'd better get back down there before she realises I've gone."

The pizza arrived thirty minutes later. Charlie devoured his in a matter of seconds, much to Susan's amazement.

"Charlie tells me you work in a fancy dress shop, Neil."

"Yeah, I'm the manager there. These two used to work with me not so very long ago, but they've both deserted the sinking ship."

"And Dorothy? You work in a bookshop?"

"Yeah, like Neil said, I used to work at the fancy dress shop too, but it wasn't for me. The bookshop is a couple of doors down from Neil's shop. I work with Molly—who you just met—briefly."

"That must be a great job. I've always thought I'd like to work in a bookshop."

"It's okay, but to be honest, a lot of the time it's boring. Most of the people who come in just want to sit around and read. Your job sounds really interesting. What sort of things will you be investigating?"

"Something that will rock Washbridge, hopefully. If any of you come across anything that you think might make a good headline, let me know."

"You mean like a vampire invasion?" Neil laughed.

Dorothy didn't.

Chapter 7

Susan was glad she'd put plenty of covers on her bed —
she'd needed them. The room had become even colder
during the night. And then there had been the constant
knocking sound. She assumed it must be the pipes, and
that it was probably connected to the heating problem.
She'd eventually fallen asleep about one o'clock.

There was no one else around when she peeked out of
her bedroom. The others obviously weren't early risers.
That was good news because it meant she wouldn't have
to wait for the shower.

By the time Susan was dressed, Dorothy was up. She
was in the kitchen, wearing a dressing gown.

"Morning!" Susan called.

Dorothy didn't look up, but did manage a grunt.

"Are you making tea?"

"Yep."

This was proving to be harder work than Susan had
hoped it might be.

"I don't suppose you could make me one while you're
at it, could you?"

Dorothy sighed. "How do you take it?"

"Milk and one sugar, please."

"You'll have to pass me the milk out of the fridge. I
don't take it."

The first thing Susan noticed when she opened the
fridge door, was that the middle shelf was empty.

"Your iron supplement's gone." She passed the milk to
Dorothy.

"Supplement? Oh yeah, it—err—it was out of date, so I
threw it away."

"Will you have to get more?"

"No. I don't need it now. I've finished the course."

"Have you been poorly?"

"No. It was just a hormone thing. Everything's back to normal now."

Dorothy pushed the cup of tea over to Susan, and then went back to staring at her phone; she made no attempt at conversation. Susan had the distinct impression that Dorothy wasn't thrilled to have her as a new flatmate, but she decided to persevere.

"What system do you guys have for sharing the housework?"

Dorothy glanced up. "Sorry?"

"The housework? I just wondered how you share it out? Do you have some sort of rota?"

"Nah, it just kind of gets done." Dorothy went back to her phone.

There was no way Susan could live with the apartment as it was. It took 'untidy' to a whole new level. There were clothes, and papers and all manner of stuff scattered everywhere. All of the surfaces looked as though they could do with dusting, and the floor needed vacuuming.

"Maybe we should have an FM," Susan suggested.

"Have a what?"

"An FM? You know, a Flatmates' Meeting. That's what we used to call it in London. Don't you call it that here?"

"I can't say I've ever heard the term."

"Don't you think it would be a good idea?"

Dorothy shrugged.

Susan decided not to press the issue. Maybe she would raise it again when all of them were together. Perhaps the two guys would be a bit more enthusiastic. They certainly couldn't be any less so.

"I suppose I'd better get going." Susan grabbed her handbag. "I'll see you tonight."

Dorothy didn't respond.

As soon as Susan had left, Dorothy hurried over to Charlie's room, and hammered on the door. "Charlie! Get up! Get out here now!"

A voice came from inside. "What's the matter? Is there a fire?"

"Just get out here now!"

She then rushed over to Neil's room, and knocked on his door. "Neil, get up!"

"Go away!"

"Get out here now!"

"What's wrong? Don't tell me you've lost your blood again."

A few minutes later, the three of them were seated in the lounge. Charlie and Neil were on the sofa; both of them still looked half asleep. Dorothy sat opposite them in the armchair.

"She's got to go!" Dorothy said.

"Who's got to go?" Neil yawned. "Are you on about that cat again?"

"Not the cat. The human! Susan whatever her name is."

"I like Susan." Charlie blinked away the sleep. "She's nice."

"Nice?" Dorothy was red in the face. "Nice?"

"I think she fancies me," Neil said.

"You think every woman fancies you."

"Why does she have to go?" Charlie said. "We've got to have a fourth flatmate. Redman said so. If we chuck her out, he'll chuck us out."

"I'll give you four reasons why she has to go. Are you both listening?"

They nodded.

"Number one: she's a human! As in, not a sup. She's the only human in the whole of this apartment block. How can we be ourselves around her?"

"I don't think it will be a problem," Charlie said.

"What about when it's a full moon? What then?"

"I usually go back to Candlefield."

"That's not the only time you turn though, is it? What about when you get really angry?"

"That doesn't happen very often."

"It only needs to happen once. If the human sees you go werewolf, what do you think she's going to do?"

"I suppose that could be awkward."

"Awkward? It would be more than awkward. And you, Neil, you can't leave the magic alone."

"That's not true."

"You're always using it. If she sees you, what do you think will happen?"

"I'll be discreet."

"Discreet?" Dorothy laughed. "You don't know the meaning of the word. And then there's reason number two: I can't keep my food in our apartment. I've had to take it upstairs to Tilly's. Every time I need blood, I have to go traipsing up there."

"It's not that far," Charlie said.

"Oh well, that's okay then." Dorothy could barely contain her anger. "So, you'd be quite happy to walk up a flight of stairs every time you wanted something to eat?"

"Well, no—"

"Exactly. And neither am I."

"You could always keep it in the bread bin." Neil laughed.

Dorothy fixed him with her gaze. "No, Neil, I can't keep my blood in the bread bin. It needs to be in *that* fridge."

"I told her it was your iron supplement," Charlie said. "She seemed to accept that."

"Maybe, but don't you think she's going to get curious sooner or later? What do you think will happen when she realises it's synthetic blood? And even if I did keep it in the fridge, I still can't drink it while she's around. And reason number three: she asked about our housework rota."

"What rota?" Neil said.

"We don't have one, do we?" Charlie said.

"Exactly. And we don't need one. There's nothing wrong with this place, but she wants to hold an FM tonight."

"Full moon?" Charlie looked puzzled.

"Not a full moon—a flatmates' meeting. Apparently, in London, that's what they do. They hold meetings to discuss housework rotas."

"I don't like that idea," Neil said.

"No, me neither," Charlie agreed. "We already keep this place tidy, don't we?"

They all nodded.

"And last but not least," Dorothy continued. "Reason number four: She's an investigative reporter, and is looking for a big story to make her name. If we don't get rid of her, *we* may turn out to be her big story."

"I still don't see how we can get her out," Charlie said.

"You need to have a word with Socky, Neil," Dorothy

said.

"I've told you. He won't move out."

"We don't want him to move out now. We want him to scare Susan to death, so she can't wait to get out of here."

Forty-five minutes later, they'd all showered and dressed.

"Do you want a lift in?" Neil shouted to Dorothy.

"No, I'm okay. I'm going to walk this morning. I need some fresh air to clear my head. Besides which, I'm starving."

After the boys had left, Dorothy made her way upstairs.

"Dorothy?" Tilly was still in her dressing gown, and looked half asleep.

"Aren't you at work today, Tilly?"

"Yeah, but it's my late start. Did you want your blood?"

"Yes, please."

"You don't need to knock. You can just let yourself in."

"I don't like to do that. Not when you're in. It doesn't seem right."

"How was your first night with your new flatmate?"

"Don't ask. She's a nightmare. She's trying to be friendly, but I gave her the cold shoulder. It didn't seem to work though. She's already decided that we've got to have a flatmate's meeting to talk about sharing the housework."

"Your place is a bit of a tip."

"No, it's not!" She looked around at Tilly's apartment, which was spotless. "You're just obsessively clean."

"No, I'm not. This is how normal people live. You three? Well, you deserve one another. Every time I come down to your apartment, I feel like I need to have a shower afterwards."

"Hey! That's a bit harsh!" She walked over to Tilly's fridge, grabbed one of the two bottles of synthetic blood, and took a long drink. "Mmm, I needed that! I usually have a drink last thing at night, but I didn't get the chance."

"You should have come up here."

"I couldn't be bothered, and besides, I didn't want to disturb you."

"You could always have drunk the human's blood."

"What?" Dorothy looked aghast.

"Why not? Flatmates share things. I'm sure she'd be more than willing to share a little of her blood with you."

"You mean kill her?"

"No! Of course not. You could just soft-feed from her."

"Do what?"

"Dorothy, I despair of you sometimes. Are you sure you're actually a vampire?"

"Of course I am."

"And you don't know what soft-feeding is?"

"No."

"Sit down."

Dorothy did as she was told. Tilly sat next to her.

"Soft-feeding is when you take a little blood from a human, but you don't bite their necks. You just drain a little, and hope they don't notice."

"How are they not going to notice you draining their blood?"

"Obviously, you don't do it while they're awake. You wait until they're asleep, and then prick a finger or toe. Let the blood drip onto a dish, and there you go. It's never going to satisfy your hunger though. You'll still need synthetic blood. But, there's nothing quite like the taste of human blood. Don't you think?"

"I don't know."

"Please don't tell me you've never tasted human blood."

"I haven't."

"Not once? Not even a drop?"

"No."

"Oh, girl, you don't know what you're missing. Synthetic blood's okay, but it's not a patch on the real thing. I have to indulge myself every now and then."

"Here in Washbridge?"

"Yeah, of course."

"You attack humans?"

"No! Haven't you been listening to a word I've said? I soft-feed on them. Sometimes I do it when I go to a human girlfriend's house for a sleepover. I wait until they're asleep, and then take a little taster."

"You've never told me this before, Tilly."

"I didn't think I needed to. It's what most vampires do in the human world. I can't believe you've never done it. Why don't we try it together tonight on your human? You could give me the nod when she's asleep, and I'll pop down."

"No!" Dorothy said. "It's too dangerous. Definitely not!"

Chapter 8

The Bugle had its own car park, which was located in the basement of the building. Susan's allocated space was as far from the stairs and lift as it could possibly have been. At least she didn't have to pay to park. Even with the lighting it was still quite dark and dingy down there.

Her footsteps echoed as she walked across the concrete floor towards the stairs. Out of the corner of her eye, she thought she saw something move. Susan stopped for a moment, but could see nothing, so carried on walking. Then it happened again; this time she heard a noise.

"Hello?" she shouted. "Is somebody there?"

There was no response, so she picked up her pace towards the stairs. She wasn't going to risk the lift in case someone jumped in with her. Suddenly, a figure stepped out from behind a pillar, and almost scared her to death. She instinctively reached into her handbag where she always kept a spray for just this kind of situation.

"Come any closer and I'll use this!"

He was a short, slight man, so Susan wasn't particularly worried. Even without the spray, she knew how to handle herself. Unless this guy had some kind of weapon, she was confident she could take him down without much difficulty.

"It's all right, Susan." The man took a step closer. "There's nothing to be worried about."

"How do you know my name? Who are you?"

"You can call me Manic."

"Manic? That's not a name."

"It's what everyone calls me." He laughed like a man possessed. The nickname made a little more sense now.

"I asked how you know my name?

"Manic knows lots of things."

In Susan's experience, people who referred to themselves in the third person were either plonkers or crazy. This guy was most probably both.

"What do you want?"

"Put the spray away, sweetie."

"Don't 'sweetie' me! What are you doing down here? This is private property."

"Manic is here to offer you his help."

"What kind of help?"

"Information. That's what you reporters thrive on, isn't it?"

"What sort of information?"

"Manic has lots of it—some good stuff, too. If there's something rotten going on in Washbridge, then Manic knows about it."

"I'm not interested. I've got work to do. You'd better get out of here or I'll call security."

"You'd be wasting your time. They won't catch Manic. You're new to the job, aren't you? You're going to need big stories. Manic knows how these things work. If you don't come up with the goods, they'll fire your backside, and get somebody else in."

Susan didn't respond, but that summed up her situation quite accurately.

"Manic has stories." His eyes were wide and dark. "Big stories, too. Corruption, murder, you name it. Manic can give them to you before anybody else even knows there's a story to be had."

"And why would you do that?" She was still keeping her distance.

"Why do you think? For cash. Manic gives you the story; you give Manic cash."

"I don't know anything about you. Why would I trust anything you say?"

"Manic needs to build your trust. Manic understands that. That's why Manic is prepared to give you the first story for free. Once you've seen the quality of the information Manic can bring you, we can sit down and talk money."

Susan was familiar with people like Manic. Some of her colleagues in London had used some rather dodgy characters to provide them with leads. But this man? She didn't want anything to do with him. He had rat-like features, and he smelled. And not in a good way.

"I'm not interested." When she started to walk away, she half-expected to hear his footsteps behind her. If she did, she'd make him sorry he'd ever shown his ugly face. But she heard nothing. When she reached the stairs, she turned around. He was nowhere to be seen.

Susan had no sooner got to her desk than Flynn called her into his office.

"Are you okay, Flynn?" He didn't look it. He looked worried.

"Not really. Take a seat, Susan."

This sounded ominous. She had a horrible feeling he was going to tell her the paper had folded before they'd even had a chance to try to turn it around. It would be just her luck to have found a new apartment, and then lose her job.

"What is it? What's wrong?"

"The only reason The Bugle has survived this long is

because it's been the only game in town. Anywhere else, the paper would have closed long ago."

"Been?"

"Yeah. That's about to change. Do you know West Chipping?"

"Of course. It's not far from here."

"The paper over there is The Chips. It's a terrible name, but not a bad paper from all accounts. Way better than The Bugle. Bigger circulation, better stories and better reporters. I've just heard that they're about to expand their operation. They're going to publish a sister paper here in Washbridge."

"Are they opening up offices here?"

"A satellite office, I'd guess. They'll feed the stories back to the main office in West Chipping. I'm not sure if they'll publish under the same name. They'll probably call it The Wash, or something equally stupid. But whatever they call it, it's competition, which is something The Bugle's never had before. This means our job just got way tougher."

Back at her desk, Susan was still trying to take in what Flynn had told her. He was right. This upped the ante considerably.

"You've heard, then?" Dougal Andrews was standing next to her desk. Susan hated the way he crept around.

"Heard what, Dougal?" She really didn't have the patience to deal with him.

"About The Chips."

"Yeah. Flynn just told me."

"I'm going to give them a call. They'll need reporters working over here. As The Bugle's top reporter, they'll snatch my hand off. Double my salary, probably."

Susan could hardly believe her ears. She wouldn't have paid Dougal Andrews in bottle tops.

"If you've got any sense, you'll come with me," Dougal continued. "This place is going to fold even quicker than I thought it would. Do you want me to put a word in for you?"

"No, thanks. I think I'll take my chances here."

It was just after two pm. The phone on Susan's desk rang.

"Susan Hall."

"Hi. Are you one of the reporters?" a man said.

"Yeah. You're through to the News Desk. How can I help you?"

"I might have a story for you."

"What's your name, please?"

"Sorry. It's Patmore, Alex Patmore. I work at Patmore Funeral Services."

"Okay?"

"I think there's something suspicious about one of the clients I've just processed, and I'd like to talk to you about it, if I can."

Clients? Processed? Susan shuddered at the thought. "Suspicious how?"

"Do you think we could meet somewhere? I'm busy today, but maybe tomorrow?"

"Sure. Do you want to come into our offices or would you prefer to meet in a coffee shop somewhere?"

"I don't really want to come into your offices. How about Coffee Triangle?"

"Won't it be a bit noisy in there?"

"You're right. How about Aroma?"

"I don't know that one, but don't worry, I'll find it. What time?"

"Say two?"

"Okay. I'll see you then."

***

Susan had decided to bite the bullet, and go see her mother. She'd deliberately chosen a time when she knew her father wouldn't be in. Flynn had said she could work her own hours, so she was going to take him at his word.

From the outside, her parents' house looked exactly the same as the last time she'd been there—almost three years ago. She hesitated at the front door; this wasn't going to be easy.

"Susan? Come in." Her mother beamed. "Why didn't you tell me you were coming? And why did you ring the bell? You know you can come straight in. Let's go through to the lounge. Do you want a drink?"

"No, I'm okay, thanks."

They sat together on the sofa.

"Is everything okay?" Her mother asked. "What are you doing back in Washbridge?"

"I've moved back here."

"What?" Her mother was clearly shocked. "Permanently?"

"As permanent as anything ever is. I've got a job up here."

"Why didn't you tell me? You must have known the last time we spoke on the phone. Where are you living?"

"I've got a flat-share just outside of Washbridge. It's the old sock factory. It's been converted into loft-style apartments."

"How long have you been living there?"

"I moved in yesterday. I've been staying in a motel."

"Why didn't you come and stay here?"

"You know why."

"Because of your dad?"

"Yeah."

"You and he will have to talk sooner or later."

"I'm happy to talk to him, Mum, but you know what he's like. He doesn't talk to me; he talks *at* me. I get that he doesn't approve of my choice of career, and doesn't like journalists, but this is my life. It has nothing to do with him."

"You're right, but your dad's obstinate. He'll come around eventually. I'm so glad you're here. What made you decide to come back?"

"The newspaper where I was working folded. I was looking around for something else, and happened to mention it to Dreams. She was the one who told me about the job."

"Dreams knows you're back?"

"Yeah, but don't blame her for not telling you. I told her not to say anything."

"What about your brothers? Do they know?"

"Nobody knows. Apart from you and Dreams."

Susan and her mother talked for a good hour. They'd always been close, which was more than could be said for her relationship with her father. Her mother tried to convince her to stay until he came home, so they could try to clear the air, but Susan wasn't ready to face him yet.

***

By the time she got back to the apartment, the other three were already there, seated in the lounge.

"Hi, you three. I'm glad I've caught you all together. I mentioned to Dorothy this morning that it might be an idea for us to hold an FM—err—sorry, a flatmates' meeting. Anyway, seeing as we're all here, maybe we could do it now. It'll only take a few minutes. There's just a few things we need to get sorted out. Is that okay?"

"Okay by me," Charlie said.

"Why not?" Neil nodded.

Dorothy grunted.

Susan took a seat. "First off, I assume each of you has your own food cupboard?" They nodded. "Is there one I could use for mine?"

"You could use the top one on the right hand side," Charlie said. "There's only a couple of old pans in there."

"They're *my* pans!" Dorothy objected.

"Yeah, but you never use them, do you?" Charlie said.

"I might, one day."

"There's plenty of room for them under the sink. You could keep them in there."

"I suppose so."

"That's settled, then," Susan said. "I'll take the top right-hand cupboard. The next thing is the fridge."

"There are only three shelves," Dorothy said. "So you're out of luck."

"Hold on," Charlie said. "I don't keep that much in the fridge. You could have half of my shelf, if you like. You take the right-hand side, and I'll take the left."

"Thanks. That's very kind." Susan was warming to Charlie—even if he did look a little intimidating.

"Same here," Neil offered. "I don't really have that much in there. We can do the same with my shelf. You have the right hand side; I'll have the left."

"That's very kind of you both. Thanks."

Dorothy was just about to stand up when Susan said, "Just a second, Dorothy. There's just one more thing, please."

"What is it?" she snapped. "I have to paint my toenails."

"It won't take long." I just wanted to talk about the housework. We've all got to live together, and I'm sure we'd all like the place to be clean and tidy. I thought I could draw up a simple rota—nothing too complicated. Who tidies the lounge area on a particular day, or who does the washing up on another day—that sort of thing. That way, we all do our fair share."

"That sounds like a good idea," Charlie said. "I don't see why not."

Dorothy looked daggers at him.

"We can give it a go," Neil said.

"Great!" Susan beamed. "I'll go and draw something up. If we can get this agreed, we can start tomorrow."

As soon as Susan had disappeared into her bedroom, Dorothy stood up, turned around, and glared first at Charlie and then at Neil.

"Traitors!"

Chapter 9

The next morning, the other three flatmates were still in bed when Susan got up. This seemed to be a pattern, but one she was quite happy with. It meant she could get in the shower without any hassle.

By the time she'd showered and dressed, the other three were up—dressed in PJs and dressing gowns. They all still looked half-asleep.

"Morning, everyone," Susan called to them.

All she got back was a series of grunts. At least the grunts from Charlie and Neil sounded friendly; the one from Dorothy, not so much. It was becoming increasingly obvious to Susan that Dorothy didn't want her there. She had no idea why, or what she'd done to upset her. Maybe Dorothy had enjoyed being the only female in the group, and felt that Susan was stepping on her toes. Whatever the reason, all Susan could do was try to be friendly, and hope that Dorothy would come around in time.

She was pleased to have caught them all together because she'd been working late into the night to produce her masterpiece.

"Hey, guys. Can I show you this?"

"What is it?" Charlie could barely keep his eyes open.

"If you could all come over to the lounge, it'll be easier to show you there."

Charlie had a mug of what looked like lukewarm tea. Neil was eating burnt toast, and Dorothy was grumbling under her breath.

When they were seated, Susan held up a sheet of paper. "This is the rota."

The three of them stared at it, bleary-eyed.

"What's that all about?" Dorothy said. "It's just a load of coloured squares."

"I can't understand it," Charlie said.

"It's quite simple, really. The four of us are colour-coded. I'm orange. Charlie, you're blue. Neil, you're purple, and Dorothy, you're red."

"Why am I red?" Dorothy scowled. "I don't like red. Can't I be orange?"

"We can probably sort the colour thing out later, but for now, let me talk you through how it works. Each column represents a day of the week: Monday, Tuesday, Wednesday, Thursday, and Friday. I thought we could all have the weekend off."

"Gee, thanks," Dorothy said.

Susan ignored the jibe. She was starting to get used to them.

"In each column, there are four squares. Each of those squares is a different task, such as: washing up, vacuuming the floors, cleaning the windows—"

"Cleaning the windows?" Dorothy looked horrified. "Those enormous things?"

"Well, yeah."

"How are we meant to clean those? Look how high they are."

"What do you do at the moment?"

The three of them shrugged.

"You've never cleaned them?"

"The landlord sent someone in a couple of months ago to do it," Charlie said. "But we've never touched them."

"I'm sure there must be something we can use," Susan pondered. "I'll give it some thought."

"Maybe we could walk on stilts," Dorothy snided.

"So, as I was saying, on each day there are four squares. Every weekday, you need to check the rota to see which square has your colour on it—that's your task for the day. So we each have only one task to do each day. That's reasonable, don't you think?"

"That doesn't sound too bad." Charlie nodded. "I think I can manage one thing a day."

"What about when someone has to go out for the day?" Neil scratched his chin. "What happens to their task then?"

"The way we used to do it, when I was in London, is that we'd arrange a swap. So, let's say I know I'm going to be out tomorrow. I'd ask one of you to swap with me. That way, you'd cover my task tomorrow, and I'd do the same for you on another day. That system seemed to work pretty well. Do you think we could do a similar thing here?"

"I suppose so," Charlie said.

Susan checked her watch. "I'm running late. I'd better get off. I'll leave this rota for you to study. If you have any questions, you can talk to me when I come home tonight."

As soon as Susan was out of the door, Dorothy rounded on the two guys. "This is all your fault. Both of you. We should have nipped this in the bud as soon as she started talking about flatmate meetings. We should have told her where she could shove her FM."

"It sounds a reasonable system to me," Charlie said.

"Oh, shut up, Charlie!" Dorothy snapped. "You're too nice for your own good!"

"Hey, Dorothy." Neil had a stupid grin on his face. "You'd better hurry up or you'll be late for work."

She glanced at the kitchen clock. "What are you talking

about? I've got plenty of time."

"Not according to this." Neil picked up the rota. "It's your turn to do the dishes, so you'd better get cracking."

She snatched the rota from him. "I don't know what you're laughing at, Neil. You're down to do the vacuuming."

***

When Susan arrived at the office, she spotted a small envelope on her desk. There wasn't an address on it—just her name. It had obviously been hand-delivered.

She turned to the man seated at the next desk. "Hey, Pete, did you see anybody drop this envelope on my desk?"

"Nobody's been near your desk since I got here. Whoever it was must have delivered it early this morning or during the night."

"Okay, thanks."

She tore it open. Inside was a grubby sheet of paper. The writing on it was barely legible. The spelling was atrocious; the grammar was non-existent.

She had to read it through a couple of times just to get the gist of it. It seemed to relate to some kind of extortion racket in Washbridge. According to the note, the perpetrators were targeting smaller shops on the eastern side of the town. It went on to say that although several of the victims had contacted the police, nothing had happened because the chief of police was being paid by the criminals to turn a blind eye.

Although she couldn't be a hundred percent certain, Susan suspected that the note had come from the creepy little man who had approached her in the basement garage. What had he called himself? Something stupid. Manic, that was it. Why would he have left her this note? Then she remembered that he'd said he was prepared to give her the first story for free, so she'd know his sources were good. An extortion scheme would be a big story in itself, but if the chief of police was implicated, that was a front-page headline if ever she'd seen one.

Dougal was standing at Bob Bragg's desk. There were a couple of other reporters there too. Susan had no interest in what they were talking about, but they were speaking so loudly that it was impossible not to hear. Dougal Andrews seemed to be bad-mouthing The Chips newspaper. She found that more than a little curious because only the day before, he'd told her that he intended approaching that paper for a job. He'd even suggested she do the same. What had changed? There could be only one explanation. They must have turned him down. He was never going to admit that he'd been kicked back; he wouldn't want to lose face. Instead, he was now telling everyone how bad The Chips was.

While the three men were still talking, Stella came over to Susan's desk.

"Are you okay, Stella? You look a bit down."

"To tell you the truth, Susan, I'm worried. I assume you've heard the news about The Chips."

"Yeah, Flynn told me."

"I think this might be the end for The Bugle. If this place folds, I'll be out of a job, and they're not easy to come by."

"Don't worry about it, Stella. The Chips doesn't even have a presence here yet. It's going to take them a while to build up a readership. That gives us plenty of time to turn things around."

"Gives *you* time," Stella said. "You and Flynn. No one else is going to do it. Look at those wastes of space." She pointed to Dougal Andrews and his entourage. "Did you know he tried to get a job at The Chips?"

"Yeah, he told me. I gather from what I just overheard, that they turned him down."

"Laughed in his face, more likely. Now he's trying to make out that they wanted him, but he decided to stay here. He's such a liar."

Later that afternoon, Susan heard footsteps approaching her desk. She looked up, fully expecting to see Dougal Andrews or Bob Bragg, but instead, she saw her youngest brother.

"Ray?" She could tell by his expression that this was not a 'welcome-back-to-Washbridge' visit.

"Mum said you were working here." He spat the words. "What are you thinking?"

"Come with me." Susan led him to one of the interview rooms, and closed the door behind them.

"Why are you working here, Susan? You know what this rag is like."

"The paper I was working for down in London folded. I needed a job. I needed money. This came up, so I applied for it. The Bugle has new owners now, and they're determined to change its image."

"Don't be so naive!" He laughed. "This paper will never change its spots. Don't you know how this makes the family look?"

"And my career doesn't count for anything? I'm sorry,

Ray, but we can't all be Dad's blue-eyed boy, can we?"

"What do you mean by that?"

"You know what I mean. You followed him into the police force, so of course you're his favourite. I committed the crime of becoming a journalist."

"Can you blame Dad? After all the problems he's had with the press?"

"That was just one rogue journalist. You can't tar us all with the same brush."

"Mum said you didn't even tell her you were coming back."

"I didn't tell anyone, and this is precisely why. I knew what kind of reception I'd get. Take it from me, I'd rather be in London, but beggars can't be choosers. I need this job."

"There's no talking to you." He started towards the door. "Just don't embarrass the family any more than you have to."

"Ray! Wait."

"What now?"

"Can I assume that if I need any help from the police, I can call on you?"

He left without another word, slamming the door behind him.

Susan was still shaking with anger, when the door opened again.

It was Stella.

"Are you okay, Susan?" She sounded concerned.

"Yeah, I'm fine."

"I could see you were arguing. Is that your ex?"

"No. That's one of my brothers. As you can tell, we're just one big, happy family."

Chapter 10

It was Charlie's day off. His mother had phoned the night before to ask if he'd pop over. His father had died when he was a teenager, leaving his mother to bring up Charlie and his younger brother, Ralph, alone.

"Hey, Mum," Charlie burst through the door.

"Charlie." His mother gave him a big hug. He hugged her right back. The bond between the two of them was plain to see. "It's lovely to see you. How are things?"

"Great, thanks. We've got a new flatmate."

"Has one of the others left?"

"No. Someone has taken the fourth room. She moved in a couple of days ago."

"She? Is she a werewolf?" His mother was always trying to play matchmaker.

"No."

"A vampire?"

"No."

"A witch, then?"

"She's a human."

"Why would you let the room to a human? I thought that apartment block was sups only."

"We didn't have any say in it. The landlord decided we were dragging our heels over getting another flatmate, so he found one for us."

"How do you all feel about that?"

"Everyone's a bit nervous because she's a reporter. If she realises who we really are, we may end up front page news."

"You have to be careful, Charlie. You know what'll happen if it comes out that you're sups, don't you?"

"The Rogue Retrievers will come after us."

"That's right. How is everyone getting along with her?"

"Neil's kind of okay with it, like me, but Dorothy isn't. She really doesn't like Susan. She wants us to try to drive her out."

"Why's Dorothy taken against her?"

"It makes life a lot more difficult for her. She normally keeps her synthetic blood in the fridge, but now Susan's there, she has to keep it at her friend's apartment, upstairs."

"How do you plan on getting the human to move out?"

"Do you remember I told you about the ghost that Neil invited in?"

"The sock man?"

"Yeah, Socky. We're kind of hoping he might scare her away, but it hasn't worked yet. Anyway, what about you, Mum? You sounded a bit upset when you called."

"It's your brother again."

"What's he done this time?"

"I don't know what's wrong with him. You were never like this when you were a teenager. You were always such a good boy."

It was during his teenage years that Charlie had lost touch with a lot of his friends. They'd all become a lot wilder, and more interested in drinking and partying. That had never appealed to Charlie. And besides, he'd always been busy around the house, helping his mother.

"What's Ralph been up to?"

"This is the worst one yet. When he came in last night, he had bruises and scratches on his arms, and his shirt was ripped. I'm pretty sure he'd let the werewolf out."

"I know he shouldn't, Mum, but at least he's in

Candlefield so he can't get—"

"That's just it. He wasn't in Candlefield. He's started going to Washbridge with some of those so-called friends of his."

"I didn't think he was allowed to go there?"

"He isn't. I told him the same as I used to tell you at that age. He isn't allowed to go there until he's eighteen, but he doesn't take any notice. He goes where he wants and does whatever he pleases. I'm worried about him, Charlie. If he goes werewolf in Washbridge, sooner or later, he's going to hurt someone, and then he's really going to be in trouble."

"I assume you've told him all of this, Mum."

"Of course I have, but I'm wasting my breath. I was hoping you could talk some sense into him."

"He won't listen to me."

"Will you at least try, Charlie? Please."

"Okay, I'll give it a go."

He went upstairs, his big feet clumping on the steps as he went. The sound of heavy metal music was coming from his brother's bedroom. Charlie knocked on the door, but there was no answer, so he pushed it open and walked in. Ralph was lying on the bed with his eyes closed. Charlie could tell he wasn't asleep because he was moving his hands in rhythm to the music. He pressed 'pause' on the iPod.

"Hey! What are you doing?" Ralph sat up. "Turn the music back on."

"We need to talk."

"No, we don't. Turn the music back on."

"I said we need to talk." Charlie sat in the chair next to the door.

"Has Mum sent you up here to have a go at me? Like she hasn't done that already?"

"Why have you been going to Washbridge?"

"Who says I have?"

"Are you denying it?"

"What if I have? What does it matter?"

"It's dangerous."

"You see danger everywhere. You've forgotten what it's like to be a werewolf."

"What are you talking about? What do you think happens to me every full moon?"

"All you ever do is come back to Candlefield, and go to the Range with all the other pseudo-werewolves."

"Pseudo? What is that supposed to mean?"

"You should stay in Washbridge—scare a few humans. Maybe even attack a few."

"Is that what you've been doing?"

"I've just been having fun. I'm not going to hurt anybody. Not much anyway."

"You're a disgrace, Ralph." Charlie stood up. "If Dad could see you now, he'd be ashamed."

"Don't talk to me about my father. I never knew him."

"Of course you did."

"No, Charlie, I didn't. Not really. The only memories I have of him are what I've seen in photographs."

"He wouldn't put up with this nonsense."

"Well, he isn't here, is he? So we'll never know."

"I know, and I'm telling you it's unacceptable."

Ralph jumped off the bed; the two of them were now face-to-face. Any moment they would turn werewolf on one another.

"Both of you! Stop it now!" Their mother was standing

in the doorway.

***

Charlie was still fuming when he left his mother's house. He had intended to stay all day, but knew if he did that, things could get really nasty. His mother had asked him over to try to make things better, not worse. There was nothing he could say to Ralph that would make any difference. Ralph was rebelling, and he wasn't about to listen to any adult, particularly not his mother, and certainly not to Charlie.

When he got back to Washbridge, Charlie met up with Doug, another werewolf, at their favourite pub, The Howling. It was one of the most popular pubs among the werewolf community in Washbridge.

He found Doug standing at the bar.

"Hey, Charlie," Doug said. "You sounded a bit stressed on the phone."

"It's that brother of mine."

"Let me get you a drink, and you can tell me all about it. The usual?"

"Yes, please."

Doug ordered a pint of bitter for himself, and a half of lager for Charlie. As the two of them sat at the bar, Charlie brought Doug up to speed.

"I wouldn't worry about it." Doug took a long drink. "I was just as bad when I was a teenager."

"I know you were. I never really went through that phase."

"You've always been a good boy." Doug laughed.

"Apart from when you're on the rugby field, of course. Then you turn into a killing machine."

"Hey, I'm not that bad!"

"Let's put it this way. I'm glad I'm on your team, and not the opposition's. I've seen some of the damage you've inflicted on our opponents."

Charlie laughed. He'd never let the werewolf out while he was on the rugby field, but he'd come close a few times. He loved rugby. He enjoyed being able to let out the aggression. On the rugby field, everybody was an animal.

After a few minutes, the two men made their way into the small room, at the back of the bar, where there was a pool table.

"Are you ready for a drubbing?" Doug grinned.

"Care for a small wager?" Charlie took out his wallet.

"A fiver a frame?"

"You're on."

Doug took the first frame easily. Charlie took the second. They were halfway through the third when a gang of young men, all in their early twenties, walked in. They were humans, and it didn't take a genius to see they'd already had way too much to drink.

"We want to play." One of them banged the pool table.

"You can have the table when we've finished this game," Doug said. "We won't be long."

"You've been on here for ages already." The tallest of the gang stepped forward.

"Only because there was no one else waiting to play," Charlie said. "Now, if you don't mind, we'd like to finish our game."

As Charlie bent down to take his shot, the tall man

nudged his arm causing him to miss the pot. Charlie turned around and grabbed the man. "I said you'll have to wait."

Suddenly, all the other young men surrounded him.

"Charlie, it's time to go," Doug shouted, but Charlie had seen the red mist. The werewolf was surging inside of him. Any moment now, he'd release it, and tear them all limb from limb.

"Charlie, we have to go!"

The next thing he knew, he was being dragged out onto the street where Doug walked him around to the back of the pub. "What on earth were you doing in there? You nearly turned."

Charlie was still a bit dazed from it all. "No, I didn't."

"I can tell when you're about to turn. Another ten seconds, and you would have gone full werewolf on them. That would have been you and me back in Candlefield, locked away by the Rogue Retrievers. I've never seen you go off like that before."

"I'm sorry. I'm really sorry. I guess it's all that stuff with Ralph. It's got me riled up."

"You'd better get off home before you do something stupid. Don't stop to talk to anyone on the way."

"Okay. Thanks for getting me out of there, Doug. I'm really sorry."

***

So much for his day off. Charlie was beginning to think he'd rather work seven days a week. At least at the gym, he got to work out his aggression and anger. Plus, there were always lots of pretty young women there. Today had been a complete write-off. He usually enjoyed going to see his mum, but the run-in with Ralph had spoiled it. And then to top it off, he'd almost lost control in the pub, and had very nearly gone werewolf on those stupid humans. There was no excuse for that. He frequently came into contact with idiots—not just humans—sups as well. But he'd always managed to keep his werewolf under control. The only time he couldn't was on a full moon. That's why he always took himself back to Candlefield—to the Range. He couldn't do any harm to anyone there. The worst he could do was get into a bit of a scrape with another werewolf. But today, in that bar, if Doug hadn't stepped in, Charlie would have turned. It would have been a bloodbath, and that would have been the end of the human world for Charlie. He would've been back to Candlefield, and probably never allowed to leave again.

When he got back to the apartment, he couldn't believe his eyes. Neil was in the lounge, laughing and joking with the brunette witch from upstairs.

"Hi, Charlie," Neil called.

Charlie could feel his anger rising again. Neil could have any woman he wanted, and knew how much Charlie liked the witch, so why would he do this?

"Hi," Charlie grunted.

"Hello there." The witch waved to him.

"Hi."

Charlie was about to make his way to his room when Neil stood up.

"Well, like I said, Amelia, I can't stay. I'm meeting someone in a few minutes."

"Okay." Amelia smiled. "Thanks for the drink."

"No problem." As Neil walked towards Charlie, he

gave him a wink. "Get in there," he mouthed.

"Aren't you going to come and join me?" Amelia called.

"Err—yes. Of course." Charlie could feel the colour rising in his cheeks as he made his way over.

"So, now I know your name, Charlie." Amelia held up a bottle of wine. "Would you like a drink?"

"Not for me, thanks. I had a drink earlier, and I've got rugby practice later."

"You play rugby?"

"Yeah." He took a seat opposite her. She was even more attractive close up.

"I do like rugby players. It's a much better game than football. Do you play often?"

"Most weekends, and we have two practice sessions in the week. What were you and Neil talking about?"

"Nothing much. I shouldn't really say this, but your friend's a bit full of himself, isn't he?"

Charlie smiled. "Yeah, he is a bit."

"To tell you the truth, I was going to say 'no' when he invited me in for a drink. He's not really my type. But then he said that you'd be back shortly, so of course I said 'yes." She looked around. "Where's your cat, by the way?"

"Pretty? She isn't actually my cat."

"I thought I saw you bring her into the apartment."

"I did, but don't let the others know."

"Your secret's safe with me." She put a finger to her lips.

"Pretty shows up most days. I give her milk and some food."

"That's probably why she turns up."

"I suppose you're right." Charlie was entranced by

Amelia's smile. "Neil's okay with it, but Dorothy hates her. She's the one who's always giving me a hard time about it. She's worried the landlord will throw us out."

"I love cats. I like it when they curl up on your lap and purr." She hesitated. "Neil told me you've taken on a human as a new flatmate. Why would you do that?"

"We didn't have any say in it. The landlord found her for us."

"I wish I'd known you were looking for someone."

"Why? Aren't you happy with your own place?"

"The flat's okay, but living with two other girls can be a bit much at times, particularly Julie. You know how vampires can be."

"Tell me about it." He grinned. "I love Dorothy, but she can be a bit of a nightmare at times."

"If the human causes you any grief, just let me know. I'll sort her out for you."

"Sort her out?"

"I could turn her into a frog."

"You can't turn Susan into a frog!"

"Okay, a kitten then. You did say you like cats."

He smiled, and hoped she was only joking.

"I suppose I'd better get going." She stood up. "This has been nice."

"Yeah, really nice."

After she'd left, Charlie began to curse himself. If he'd had just an ounce of Neil's confidence, he would have asked Amelia out on a date. But he didn't; he was too scared of making a fool of himself. No matter what anyone else might say, he knew that someone as pretty as Amelia would never go out with a big klutz like him.

Thirty minutes later, he was in his bedroom—still

daydreaming about Amelia, when a knock on his door brought him back to earth.

"Charlie? Are you in there?" It was Susan.

"Yeah. Come in."

"I'm sorry to bother you. Do you happen to know where Neil is?"

"He said he was going to meet someone."

Susan spotted the two thimbles on the cupboard.

"My mother has a huge collection of thimbles. When I was a kid, she would never let me go anywhere near them because she was scared I'd break them."

Charlie looked on in horror as she walked over to the cupboard. He was petrified that she'd look through the magnifying glass, and see the fairies.

"Why do you have this magnifying glass here?" She peered through it. "Oh I see. It lets you see the detail of the thimbles much better. These are really beautiful, aren't they? They look just like real houses. My mother would love them. You'll have to tell me where you got them from, so I can buy one for her."

"Err—they were a present." Charlie stuttered. "I'm not sure where they were from."

"And what's that? Is it a microphone?"

"That? Oh, I just threw that on there." Charlie managed to glance over Susan's shoulder at the magnifying glass. There was no sign of Greta or Bunty—they must have gone out somewhere. That was a close call.

Susan reached out as though she was about to pick up one of the thimbles.

"Could I—?"

"No!" Charlie grabbed her hand. "Sorry, I'd rather you didn't touch them. They're very fragile."

"Oh? Okay, sure. I do like them, though. If you can find out where they're from, I'd be very interested in buying one."

Chapter 11

The next day, when Susan arrived at Aroma, she was able to pick out Alex Patmore even though he hadn't given her a description of himself. He had a pale complexion and a haunted look about him. The only surprise was that he was a lot younger than she'd expected—perhaps only a couple of years older than herself. For some reason, she'd pictured him as being in his fifties.

He'd chosen a seat at the back of the café, away from the other customers.

"Alex?"

"That's me."

"Would you like another drink?"

"No, I'm okay, thanks."

She ordered a cappuccino, and then took the seat opposite him.

"Have you been doing this job long?" She regretted the crass question as soon as it had passed her lips.

"My father was a funeral director, and his father before him. I always swore I'd never join the family business, but then I struggled to get a job after uni, so here I am five years in. It's not that bad. Most of the time, anyway."

"When you called yesterday, you mentioned that you thought something was suspicious about one of the—err—clients that you'd had to—err—process?"

"In this line of business, the worst thing that can happen, apart from having to deal with a young child's death, is when you come across someone you know. Because I'm relatively young that hasn't happened—or at least it hadn't until a couple of weeks ago."

"A friend?"

"Not exactly. More of an acquaintance. The guy's name was Chris Briggs. He was homeless. I saw him most mornings on my way into work. He used to sleep in the doorways of the empty shops on Bridge Street."

"Near the bus station?"

"That's right. I take the bus into work every day. I have a flat out in Smallwash. If I was running early, we'd sometimes chat, and I'd give him a few coins for a cup of tea, or food for his dog, Pedro."

"How did he end up on the streets? Do you know?"

"He didn't talk about it much, but from what I could gather, he'd been thrown out of his family home not long after he left school. He had a drink problem—possibly drugs too. I'm not sure."

"How did he die?"

"According to the report, he threw himself off the multi-storey car park in town."

"Suicide?"

"That's what the police say."

"But I take it you don't think that's what happened?"

"There's no way Chris would have killed himself."

"But, surely if he was living on the streets—"

"He must have been depressed? You might think so, but you'd be wrong. Chris was one of the most positive people I knew. Whenever I spoke to him, he always cheered me up. And that's not the only reason I don't believe he topped himself."

Susan waited while Patmore took a drink of his coffee.

"He would never have left Pedro. He thought the world of that dog."

"Did you mention any of this to the police?"

"Yes, I told them what I've just told you."

"What did they say?"

"Not much really. I got the impression that he was little more than a nuisance to them. Chris was a homeless drunk. They weren't going to spend any time investigating what was probably nothing anyway. As far as they're concerned, he jumped—case closed."

"But you obviously still have doubts."

"Yes, I do. I thought if I could convince you that there's a story to be had, maybe you could get to the bottom of what really happened. What do you think? Is it something that you might be interested in following up?"

"I don't know. There isn't much to go on. If you can tell me everything you know about Chris Briggs, I'll certainly check it out, but I can't promise anything."

***

After she'd left the coffee shop, Susan decided to drop in on Jess Parks, one of her best friends from her pre-uni days. Jess, Susan and Dreams had been inseparable at that time. Jess was very different from Dreams who was always away with the fairies. Jess was much more grounded, and always spoke her mind. Susan hadn't seen Jess since she'd moved to London, but they spoke regularly on the phone. Even so, Jess had no idea that Susan was back in Washbridge.

Jess worked in a travel agent's just outside the city centre. Susan had wondered if she ought to phone ahead, but in the end decided to take her chances. As soon as she walked in, she spotted Jess at a desk near the back of the shop. There was no one with her, so Susan walked over, and sat in the chair in front of Jess's desk. Jess looked up from the computer screen.

"How can I help—Susan? What are you doing here?"

"Surprise!"

"Why didn't you tell me you were coming up? Are your parents okay?"

"Yeah, everybody's fine. I'm actually back to stay. I've got a job in Washbridge."

"Really? Doing what?"

"Investigative reporter for The Bugle."

"I'm gobsmacked. I never thought you'd leave London—still less come back to this dump. What went wrong?"

"The paper I was working at folded. It was Dreams who told me about this job, actually."

"Dreams? I saw her the other day. She never mentioned it. Just wait until I see her again."

"Don't give her a hard time. I made her promise not to tell anyone. The only reason she knows is because she was the one who told me about the job. I didn't even tell my mum and dad."

"Fair enough. Anyway it's great to have you back. Where are you living?"

"I'm flat-sharing with three others. Do you remember the old sock factory?"

"Yeah. Didn't they convert it into apartments?"

"That's right. I've only just moved in. Before that, I was staying in a grotty old motel."

"You're an idiot then. Why didn't you call me? I could have put you up."

"I should've done. I just didn't want Mum and Dad to find out."

"Anyway, never mind all that. This deserves a night out to celebrate the gang being back together. You, me and Dreams. What do you think?"

"I suppose so, but I don't imagine any of our old haunts are still going, are they?"

"A few, but there are some better ones now. We can get hammered, just like we used to."

"I don't think so. My days of getting hammered are well and truly behind me."

"Have you seen Tony?"

The question took Susan by surprise. Tony had been her boyfriend for a couple of years before they'd won places at different universities. They'd made a promise to stay faithful to one another, but it hadn't quite panned out that way. Susan had kept her part of the bargain, but before the first year was up, Tony had met someone else. Susan had been devastated at the time. She hadn't seen or spoken to him since, and had assumed that he was still with Lisa, the girl he'd met at university. She hadn't expected him to come back to Washbridge. He'd always sworn he never would.

"Tony's in Washbridge? You never mentioned it when we spoke on the phone."

"I didn't see any point, but now you're back, I figured you should know. He and that cow, Lisa, broke up about a year after they finished uni."

"I had no idea."

"They were living in Birmingham, but after the split, he came back here."

"Do you see him often?"

"Not really. On the few occasions I have, he's done his best to avoid me. I think he's a bit embarrassed."

"So you've never spoken to him?"

"Only once—not long after he came back. I'd probably had a bit too much to drink that night, and I laid into him. I let him know what I thought about him, and the way he'd treated you."

"You shouldn't have done that."

"I know, but I was the wrong side of merry at the time. He didn't say much. He just stared at his feet, mumbled something, and then wandered off. You're well shot of him. Are you seeing anyone at the moment?"

"Not to speak of."

"Me neither. We'll have to see what we can do about that." Jess gave her that wicked smile that Susan remembered so well. "I'd better get back to work. The boss here has a stick up his backside. He doesn't like us to talk to friends during business hours."

"Sure. Sorry, Jess. I didn't mean to get you into trouble. We'll arrange a night out sometime."

***

Not long after Susan had arrived back at the apartment, Charlie left to go to rugby practice. Neil and Dorothy were also out. Susan was actually relieved to have the place to herself. She was ready for some downtime.

She decided to rest up in the lounge for a while. Once she'd got her breath back, she'd have a shower, get changed, and make herself something to eat. At least, that had been the plan. Within five minutes of sitting down, she was fast asleep.

Fifteen minutes later, when Dorothy arrived home, she

found Susan asleep on the sofa. She quickly checked the other rooms; there was no sign of Charlie or Neil.

What did human blood taste like? Dorothy wondered. Could it possibly be as good as everyone said? Most of her vampire friends had tried it at least once, but she never had. Her mum had been very strict, and told her she must never try it because once she did, she'd always crave more. But surely once wouldn't hurt?

Dorothy remembered what Tilly had said about soft-feeding. She didn't need to bite Susan's neck. She could just prick her finger, and draw a few drops of blood onto a saucer. Just enough so she could taste it for the first time. She went into her bedroom, and found her sewing kit, from which she took the smallest needle she could find. After getting a saucer from the kitchen, she crept into the lounge where she knelt next to the sofa. Dorothy held the saucer underneath Susan's hand, then took the needle, and pressed it into her middle finger.

Susan jumped up. "Ouch! What the—?" She saw the blood on the tip of her middle finger. "What are you doing?" She glared at Dorothy, who was kneeling on the floor, with a saucer in one hand and a needle in the other. "What's going on, Dorothy?"

"Err—nothing. When I came in, you didn't stir. Not even when I spoke to you. I thought—err—I thought you were dead."

"Dead?"

"Yeah. I couldn't see you breathing, so—err—I got a needle, and stuck it in your finger to check if you were alive."

"You couldn't just shake me? Or shout at me?"

"I'm sorry. I don't know what I was thinking." She

scurried off into her bedroom.

Susan sucked the blood from her finger, and said under her breath, "That woman must really hate me."

Chapter 12

The next morning, Dorothy had set her alarm to go off early because she wanted to be out of the apartment before Susan was up. She couldn't face the embarrassment of seeing her after what had happened the night before. She cringed when she recalled the excuse she'd come up with: *'I thought you were dead.'* What had she been thinking? But then, what else could she have said? The woman must now think Dorothy was crazy, or evil, or both.

She was absolutely starving, so she called in at Tilly's on her way out.

Tilly answered the door, still half asleep.

"Dorothy? What time do you call this?"

"Sorry. I know it's early, but this is an emergency. Can I get some of my blood?"

"Of course, you know where it is."

Dorothy hurried through to the kitchen, grabbed one of the bottles, and downed half of it in one go.

"You'll give yourself a bad stomach." Tilly switched on the kettle. "Do you want a cup of tea?"

"Yeah, go on then. It's not like I don't have plenty of time."

"What are you doing up at this hour, anyway? You don't start work for another couple of hours, do you?"

"I know. Make the drinks, and I'll tell you all about it."

Tilly poured them both a cup of tea, and they went through to the lounge.

"It's all your fault anyway," Dorothy said.

"Me? What did I do?"

"You were the one who told me about soft-feeding."

Tilly laughed. "What have you done?"

"Last night when I came home from work, the guys were out, and Susan was asleep on the sofa."

"Was she now?" Tilly smiled a knowing smile.

"I remembered what you'd said about the soft-feeding, so I thought I'd give it a try while there was no one else around. I was going to draw a little blood onto a saucer, so I could have a taste. Just to see what all the fuss was about."

"What do you think of the real thing?"

"That's just it. I didn't get to taste it because when I stuck the needle into—"

"Hold on! You used a *needle*?"

"Yeah."

"I bet she screamed the place down, didn't she?"

"Yeah. She woke up, and there I was, kneeling next to her with a needle in my hand. When she saw the blood dripping from her finger, she was not best pleased."

"I'll bet." Tilly was crying with laughter. "Why on earth did you prick her with a needle?"

"That's what you told me to do."

"No, I didn't. I said you had to prick her finger while she was asleep, but I never said you should use a needle. You should have used a soft-stab."

"A what?"

"Come on, Dorothy! You really need to go back to vampire school. You must have heard of a soft-stab. It's a little gadget like the ones people with diabetes use when they need to test their blood sugar. You just put it to the finger, tap the end, and it pricks the skin, but it does it very gently. You barely feel it. Whenever I've used it, the human has never stirred. You don't get a whopping great needle, and stick it into their finger!"

Dorothy held her head in her hands. "What have I done?"

"What happened after she woke up?"

"What do you think? She wanted to know what on earth I was doing."

"I can't wait to hear how you explained that away."

"I said I thought she was dead, so I stuck a needle in her finger to see if she was alive."

Tilly was unable to speak for laughter.

"It's not funny!"

Eventually, Tilly managed to compose herself again. "Seriously? You actually said you were checking to see if she was dead?"

"It was the best I could come up with. What was I meant to say? I could hardly say, *'I'm a vampire, and I wanted to taste your blood,'* could I?"

"I suppose not. So what happened after that?"

"I went to my bedroom, and didn't come out again until this morning. That's why I got up so early; I didn't want to bump into her."

"You're going to have to face her sooner or later."

"I know, but if I can stay out of her way for a while, maybe she'll forget."

"Oh yeah. Like that's going to happen. She's not likely to forget you sticking a needle into her finger, is she?"

"You're not helping, Tilly."

***

When Neil got up, Susan was already seated at the breakfast bar.

"Morning, Susan."

"Hi."

"Are you okay?"

"Yeah. Look, what's with Dorothy?"

"How do you mean?"

"I get the distinct impression she doesn't want me here."

"I'm sure that's not true. I know she can be a bit blunt at times, but—"

"It's not that. I can handle the snide. She's acting really weird towards me."

"How do you mean?"

"Last night, I'd fallen asleep on the sofa, and then a stabbing pain in my finger woke me up. Dorothy was kneeling next to me. She'd stuck a needle into my finger, and made it bleed."

"Are you sure you didn't dream it?"

"Of course I'm sure. My finger was bleeding, and Dorothy had the needle in her hand. She said she was checking to see if I was dead."

Neil laughed. "Oh, dear."

"It's not funny."

"Sorry. I'm sure she didn't mean anything by it. Dorothy can just be a bit weird at times. You'll get used to her."

***

While she was at Tilly's, Dorothy decided she couldn't face going into work, so she phoned her boss to say she was feeling under the weather. Instead, she paid a visit to her mother, Dolly, in Candlefield.

"Dorothy? I didn't know you were coming over today. Give me a hug."

Babs, Dorothy's dog, came charging to the front door, and leapt on both of them.

"Get down, Babs," Dolly said, but the dog was so excited to see Dorothy, that it took no notice. Dorothy knelt down and let Babs lick her face. "Is everything okay?"

"Yeah. I'm just having a day off work. Why don't I take Babs for a walk, and then we can have a drink? If I don't take her first, we'll never get any peace."

"Okay. Do you want me to come with you?"

"You walk her enough, Mum. Have a rest. I'll phone you when we're on our way back, and you can put the kettle on."

"Okay then."

Dorothy put Babs' lead on, and they set off to the park. As soon as they got there, Dorothy spotted a familiar face. It was Jill Gooder, the P.I. who had helped her move to Washbridge. Jill had her dog, Barry, with her. The two dogs were soon chasing one another around and around.

"Hello, stranger," Jill said.

"I see Barry's as crazy as ever."

"Tell me about it. How are you, anyway? How's the fancy dress business?"

"I chucked that in."

"Really? I thought you liked it there."

"It was okay, but working with the same people you live with turned out not to be such a great idea. We saw way too much of one another. They were beginning to drive me crazy."

"You get on with them though, don't you?"

"Neil and Charlie? Yeah, they're okay, but only in small doses. Particularly Neil. I'm working in a bookshop a few doors down from the fancy dress shop now."

"Are you enjoying it?"

"Yeah. It can be a bit quiet at times, but it's still better than working with those two. What about you? Are you still doing your private investigator stuff?"

"Yep. Same old, same old. You're still living in the same apartment I take it?"

"Yeah. It's been great, but—" She hesitated.

"But?"

"Until now, it's just been me, Charlie, and Neil, but the landlord insisted we took on a new flatmate. She moved in a few days ago. Her name is Susan."

"Don't you like her?"

"It's not that. She's a human."

"Is that a problem?"

"Everyone in that apartment block is a sup; that's always been part of the appeal. We were able to be ourselves there. Now that we've got a human living with us, everything's changed. It's terrible. I can't even keep my synthetic blood in the fridge anymore."

"Oh dear." Jill laughed. "I can see how that might be a problem. How are you coping?"

"I have to keep it in a friend's fridge—she lives on the next floor. It's a real pain. And then last night, I made a right fool of myself."

"Go on."

"Tilly, that's my friend from upstairs—she's always telling me how good human blood tastes."

"Oh, Dorothy. Please tell me you didn't."

"I would never bite a human. But I did stick a needle in

Susan's finger while she was asleep."

"Didn't that wake her up?"

"Yeah. She screamed the place down. And now, she thinks I'm completely crazy."

"You can't blame her for that."

"That's not all. She's a reporter at The Bugle. If she realises who we really are, we'll be front page news."

Jill waved away that suggestion. "I wouldn't worry about that. The reporters at The Bugle wouldn't know a good news story if it bit them on the backside. You've nothing to worry about there."

***

"I've got a surprise for you," Dolly said when Dorothy came back from taking Babs for a walk.

"Oh?" Dorothy was always a little wary of her mother's surprises. They rarely turned out to be good.

"The thing is, I know how much you miss Babs."

"I do. Every day."

"And I know you can't have dogs in the apartment."

"It's against the terms of the lease."

"But you did say that you're allowed to keep caged birds."

Dorothy was getting bad vibes.

"Come see what I've got for you." Dolly led the way through to the back room. There, in a silver cage, was a yellow bird.

"It's a canary." Dorothy stared in disbelief.

"I was going to get you a budgie, but when I saw this beautiful yellow bird, I knew you'd love it."

Dorothy forced a smile. She'd never been a fan of caged

birds, but she could see how excited her mother was, and didn't want to throw kindness in her face. "You want me to take this back to Washbridge with me?"

"You'll be able to manage it on the bus, won't you?"

"I suppose so."

***

"A single to Washbridge, please," Dorothy said, as she climbed onto the bus.

"What about the bird?" The driver took miserable to a whole new level.

"What about it?"

"You can't get on unless you pay for that too."

"I have to pay for the bird?"

"Yep. All animals have to be paid for."

"Is it half fare?"

"Nope, full fare for both of you."

"Great." Dorothy paid the driver.

"I'm really excited," the bird said, once they'd taken their seat.

Dorothy stared at it. "How come I can understand what you're saying? I thought that animals could only talk to witches and wizards."

"That's normally the case, but your mother got one of her friends, a level six witch, to cast a spell so that I'd be able to talk to you, but only you."

"She never mentioned it."

"She wanted it to be a surprise. I wasn't supposed to tell you until we were back at your place, but I'm so excited to be going to the human world. My name's Bob, by the way. What's yours?"

"Dorothy."

"Where is it we're going, exactly?"

"To Washbridge. I have an apartment there."

"Is it big?"

"Yeah, very."

"Thank goodness for that. That place of your mother's is a bit poky. I trust you'll let me out to have a fly around?"

"I don't know about that. I'm not sure my flatmates would approve."

"Go on, Dorothy, you can't keep me locked up in this little cage all the time. What about when they're out? Surely you can let me have a fly around then?"

"I suppose so. But only when there's no one else in."

"Good, and what about the talent?"

"The talent?"

"You know—the female birds. Are there any in the vicinity?"

"You mean other canaries?"

"Canaries, budgies—I don't really mind as long as they're fit."

"Err—I don't know."

"You'd better find out, and quick, because Bob is a love machine—if you know what I mean."

Dorothy struggled up the stairs to the apartment. She had the cage in one hand and the stand in the other. Charlie was sitting in the lounge.

"What have you got there?" he asked when he spotted the cage.

"It's an elephant. What does it look like?"

"Why have you got it?"

"Mum gave it to me to make up for missing my dog.

You're not going to give me grief about it, are you?"

"No, but I am allergic to feathers. They make me sneeze, so I'd better keep my distance."

☐

Chapter 13

Neil would much rather have been going into work. It was the one day of the month that he dreaded; the day he went to Candlefield to see his parents. When he'd first moved to Washbridge, he'd visited them every week. He couldn't imagine doing that now. He'd gradually managed to extend the time between visits, initially to once a fortnight, then every three weeks, and now to the point where it was just once a month. Even that was too often, and seemed to come around much too quickly. It was always the same—they criticised—he listened.

"Neil, come on in." His father greeted him at the door. He was a tall man—much taller than Neil. "How are you doing, young man?" His father gave him a slap on the back. He was a man's man: well-built, and very athletic. He was nothing like Neil, who always felt a bit of a wimp in his father's presence. His father had been very sporty in his youth, and still managed to play tennis and golf. Neil had never shown much interest in sports, even though his father had tried to encourage him.

"You're just in time," his mother said. "Dinner will be ready in a few minutes. Go through to the dining room. Jackie and Michael are already here."

Neil's heart sank. Jackie and Michael were his siblings— both older than Neil. He normally saw them once or twice a year, which was often enough. His parents hadn't told him that they'd be there today.

"Hi, Neil!" Michael had a similar physique to their father. And like their father, he was also very sporty.

"Hey, Neil." His sister, Jackie, was also taller than Neil. She too played a host of different sports. "Come and sit next to me."

"I didn't realise you two were going to be here." Neil took a seat next to his sister.

"We thought it would be a nice surprise." Jackie grinned. "You're pleased to see us, aren't you?"

"Of course," Neil lied. "I'm always pleased to see you."

It was the best food Neil had had all month, but even that couldn't compensate for what was no doubt to come. He knew it was only a matter of time.

As it turned out, they managed to get all the way through the meal before the first salvo began.

"So, Neil," his father said. "Are you still working at that silly fancy dress shop?"

Neil hated his father's disparaging remarks. "Yes. I'm the manager there now."

"Manager?" his father laughed. "How many people actually work there?"

"Just the two of us at the moment—me and Debs. But I'm looking for someone else."

"So there's just one person under you? Not really a manager's job then, is it?"

Neil didn't respond.

"Don't you fancy a change?" his mother said. "Something a little more challenging."

"I'm perfectly happy where I am. The money is okay, and the customers are fun. Most of the people who come into the shop are planning a party, so they're usually in a good mood. I enjoy it."

"Come on, Neil!" His brother laughed. "You can do better than that."

"Look, Michael, do we have to do this every time we're together? I don't tell you how to run your life. I don't tell

Jackie how to run hers. Why do you all feel the need to tell me how to run mine?"

"Because you're wasting yours," his father said. "Jackie and Michael have worked their butts off to get to level five, and it's only a matter of time before they join your mother and I on level six."

"So that's what this is all about." Neil took a drink of his lemonade. "I've told you all before. I'm not as interested in magic as you are."

"Not interested in magic?" His father thumped the table. "You're a wizard. What kind of wizard isn't interested in magic? You do realise how this makes us look, don't you?"

"Here we go. You can't bear the thought that your son is only on level three, can you? What does it matter?"

"Of course it matters." His father was becoming redder and redder in the face. His mother put her hand on her husband's to try to calm him down. Neil's father took a deep breath and continued. "Look, we all know you struggled with magic, and that it's taken you longer than expected to get to level three."

"By 'longer than expected,' you mean longer than it took any of you."

"Yes, but you got there in the end. That's what matters. And if you'd carried on, you would have been at the same level as your brother and sister by now."

"I don't care about any of that, Dad. We've been over this a thousand times. I don't want the same things as you, Mum, or Michael and Jackie. I'm very pleased that you've achieved such a high level. But it's not for me."

"Your father and I have been talking," his mother said. "We know money's tight, but we thought that if you came back to Candlefield — "

"I'm not coming back, Mum."

"Just hear me out. If you came back, we could support you for a few years so that you could concentrate solely on your magic studies. If you had no other distractions, and you didn't have to work, then we're sure you could make it to level five."

"It's very kind of you and Dad to offer, but I don't want your money. I have no interest in progressing beyond level three. That's good enough for me."

"Good enough?" His father thumped the table again.

"What's wrong with you, Neil?" Michael chipped in. "You're a level three wizard living in the human world doing a no-mark job."

"It's nice to know what you all really think of me." Neil stood up. "I guess I should leave you magical supremoes to it. You won't want a lowly level three wizard in your presence."

"Wait, Neil," his mother called after him, but it was too late. Neil had already stormed out of the house, slamming the door behind him.

Back in Washbridge, he needed to cheer himself up after that encounter, so he went to one of his favourite bars, Candy Time. The place was always quieter in the daytime. After ordering a beer, he spotted two young women standing at the far side of the bar. Neil might not be a level five wizard, but level three magic was good enough for his purposes. It had always served him well when trying to impress the ladies. All humans loved magic — or at least so it seemed. Neil was so much better than the average 'magician' because of course he was performing *real* magic.

He engaged his trademark smile as he approached the two women. "Hello there, ladies!"

One of them was a blonde — the other a brunette. They both eyed him suspiciously.

"Do you like magic?"

"Err — yeah," the brunette said. "I guess so."

"Why don't I show you some? Here, let me have your watch."

She pulled her arm away.

"I'm not going to steal it. I just want to show you a little magic. Don't you trust me?"

"This was a present from my parents," the brunette said. "How do I know you won't run off with it?"

"I tell you what —" Neil reached inside his pocket. "Here's my wallet. Take a look inside. My credit cards and cash are in there. Hold on to that, and let me have your watch. I'm not going to run off and leave my wallet behind, am I?"

That seemed to satisfy the young woman who slipped off the silver wristwatch, and passed it to him. Neil put it on the bar, then took a few steps back so that he couldn't reach it.

"Keep your eyes on the watch."

The two women stared intently at it.

"Are you ready?"

They nodded.

"Okay, three, two, one." Neil cast the 'hide' spell, and the watch became invisible to the two women. It was actually still on the bar, but they couldn't see it.

"Wow, how did you do that?"

"I'm a wizard." He laughed.

"You haven't lost my watch, have you?" The brunette sounded a little worried.

"No, of course not. You still have my wallet, don't you?"

She held it up.

"Okay, three, two, one." He reversed the spell, and they could once again see the watch. "There you go. Good as new."

The young woman slipped the watch back on her wrist, and handed Neil his wallet.

"And now, as payment for the magic show, you both have to give me your phone number."

By the time he left the bar, he was feeling much better about himself. Neil had no desire to pursue magic beyond level three, but at times like this, he did enjoy being a wizard. He'd just earned himself a phone number. The blonde already had a boyfriend, but the brunette had seemed quite open to the idea of meeting up with him again. That was how he often found his girlfriends. He dazzled them with his magic and charm.

***

When Neil arrived back at the apartment, Charlie and Dorothy were sitting in the lounge. Charlie was reading the newspaper; Dorothy was studying her phone. Just then, the canary cheeped.

"What the —?" Neil stared at the bird.

"It's mine." Dorothy stood up.

"What's it doing here?" Neil walked over to the cage.

"It's a present from my mother. She knew that I'd been missing Babs, so she bought Bob for me."

"Bob? What kind of a name is Bob for a self-respecting canary? How are you doing, Bob?"

The canary cheeped at Neil.

"Why won't he speak to me?"

Dorothy shrugged. She didn't want the others to know that Bob could talk to her, and only her. On the bus ride home it had occurred to her that the canary could act as her eyes and ears when she was out.

"You're not thinking of keeping him here, are you?" Neil said.

"Why not? He isn't doing any harm."

"Hmm? We'll see about that. Anyway, what's this I hear about you attacking our new flatmate?"

"I didn't attack her. What did she say to you?"

"That you pricked her finger."

"Well, yes, I did do that."

"You did what?" Charlie looked genuinely shocked. "Why would you do that?"

"It was all a misunderstanding," Dorothy said. "Tilly told me that vampires often soft-feed off humans without them noticing."

"Soft-feed?" Neil looked puzzled. "What does that mean?"

"It's when you don't bite their necks to drink their blood. You just prick their finger, and let a few drops drip onto a saucer."

"So you pricked Susan's finger?"

"Yes, but Tilly didn't make it clear that I should have used a special device called a soft-stab. I just used a needle from my sewing kit."

"Oh dear!" Charlie laughed. "What did Susan do?"

"She woke up and looked at me like I was insane.

Hardly surprising, seeing as how I was kneeling on the floor next to her with a needle in my hand."

"Where is she, anyway?" Neil looked around.

"She's not back from work yet," Dorothy said. "I'm not looking forward to seeing her. I feel a bit embarrassed after what happened yesterday."

"A bit? If I'd just attacked someone with a needle, I'd feel more than a *bit* embarrassed."

"You're not helping, Neil!"

Chapter 14

On her way into the multi-storey car park, where Chris Briggs had met his untimely death, Susan stopped to study the sign next to the entrance. The roof and fifth floor were reserved for employees of the town council whose offices adjoined the car park. The floors below those were operated by a private company, and were open to the public.

"Hi." Susan put on her best smile for the security man who was busy crushing candy on his phone.

He grunted something, but didn't look up.

"I'm from The Bugle."

"You want to get that crossword sorted out." He put his phone onto the table in front of him.

"Sorry?"

"The crossword. I used to be able to do it, but now they've gone and made it too difficult. You need to get it sorted."

"Okay. I'll have a word. Can I ask you about the man who fell from the roof?"

"He didn't fall. He jumped."

"Do you have CCTV?"

"Up to the fourth floor, yeah."

"What about the floors above that?"

"Nah. They belong to the council. They haven't got any cameras up there—cheapskates."

"So the suicide wasn't caught on CCTV?"

"Nah, like I said, there's no cameras up there. But it's obvious that's what happened, isn't it?"

"How do you mean?"

"The guy was a loser. He didn't have a pot to—"

"I get the picture."

"Did the police view the CCTV for the floors below the fifth floor, to see how he got up to the roof?"

"Yeah, but he wasn't on it."

"How do you mean?"

"What I said. He wasn't on it."

"So how did he get up there?"

"The cameras on the south stairs are out. The cops reckon he must have gone up that staircase."

"Which are the south stairs?"

"Around the back." He pointed.

"I didn't even realise there were stairs around there. Why would he have gone around there when there are three other sets of stairs on the front and sides of the building?"

The man shrugged and went back to his phone. Candy Crush was obviously calling.

"Okay, thanks for your time." Susan started for the door.

"Don't forget to get the crossword sorted."

Susan simply didn't buy any of that. Coming from Bridge Street, which was where Chris Briggs had spent most of his time, the last staircase he would have been likely to use was the south one. It struck her that that was just a convenient get-out for the police who didn't then have to worry about how he'd really ended up on the roof.

***

"Great!" Susan said, under her breath. This was all she needed today. She'd only been at her desk for a few minutes when she spotted Margie coming through the door at the far end of the office. She was already making a beeline for Susan's desk. Dougal Andrews had a big smirk on his face.

"Hello, Margie." Susan had to force a smile.

"I hope you don't mind me calling in again, but I really would like to get this thing moving if we can. Who knows how many more people have already been taken back to Candlefield?"

"If you recall, Margie, I did say that I've only just started in the job, and it might take me a while to get around to this."

"But Susan, it's so important."

"If there were so many people disappearing, surely we'd have heard about it, wouldn't we?"

"Not necessarily. Most of those partners who have been left behind have been brainwashed."

"Brainwashed?"

"Yeah. That's what they do. They brainwash you, so you'll forget."

"Who are *they*?"

"The supernaturals, of course. The Rogue Retrievers. I don't think the brainwashing can have worked on me, though. Sometimes I wish it had because then I wouldn't have to face all this ridicule. Everybody thinks I'm crazy, but I'm not. It's all true. Please, Susan, if you'd just follow up on this story, you'll make a name for yourself. You'll be famous."

Infamous, more like. Susan needed to shut this down once and for all. But if she just sent Margie away again, she'd no doubt be back the next day, and the next. Maybe if she allowed Margie to get it off her chest, that would satisfy her.

"I tell you what, Margie. How about we go back to your house? You can give me all the details, and I can take it from there."

"Would you, Susan?" Margie's face lit up. "That would be great. I've been trying to get someone to listen to me for so long. You don't know what this means to me." She threw her arms around Susan, and hugged her.

Dougal and Bob were in hysterics.

Susan gently pulled away. "How did you get here today, Margie?"

"I came on the bus."

"Okay, we'll take my car."

Margie's house was not far from where Susan's parents lived. It was an area of Washbridge that Susan knew well. The house was just like all the others on the street. There was nothing about it to suggest that a nutjob lived there.

Margie led the way inside. "I'll make us both a cup of tea. How do you take yours, Susan?"

"Milk and one sugar, please."

While Susan drank her tea, Margie busied herself collecting photos and papers, which she then arranged carefully on the coffee table.

"How would you like to do this?" Margie asked.

"Perhaps you should start by telling me something about your husband. I don't even know his name."

"This is Gary." Margie held up a photograph of herself with a man who was a good six inches taller than her. He had black hair and a winning smile. The two of them looked very happy together. "This was taken about a year before they took him away."

"Had you been together long?"

"We were school sweethearts. We were together almost thirty-five years."

"Do you have children?"

"Yes, two girls. Well, I say girls, but they're women now. They both live in this street."

"Really?" Susan couldn't imagine living in the same street as her parents.

"Gary doted on the girls. He inherited some money from his parents, and used it to buy houses for them. I'm not sure either of them would have chosen to live here, but they weren't going to refuse the offer of a house. Willow lives at number thirty-two, and Rose, my older girl, lives at forty-one."

"I see. Why don't you start at the beginning?" Susan knew that if she wanted to put an end to this charade, she was going to have to listen to Margie's ludicrous story in full.

"Like I said, we'd known each other since our school days. I always thought his parents were a little strange. They were never very keen on me for some reason. It was much later, after I'd discovered that Gary was a wizard, that he told me his parents had been supernaturals too. They hadn't wanted him to marry a human. It wasn't that they didn't like me; they just wanted him to marry a sup."

"A sup? That's a paranormal creature, right?"

"Yeah. A wizard or a witch, or a vampire. Or even a werewolf."

"So when did you first notice something unusual about Gary?"

"Even before we were married, there were little things. I remember I had a glass ornament which my mother bought for me. It was a little ballerina. One day, I knocked it onto the floor and it smashed. But the next thing I knew, Gary handed it back to me, and it was as good as new. When I asked him how he'd done it, he just laughed and said, *'It's magic.'* I knew it was weird, but I was just pleased to have my ballerina back. There were other little things, too. One day we were out somewhere, and it was really hot. I remember telling Gary that the heat was making me feel ill, and then, just a few seconds later, it started to rain."

"Surely that's not so unusual. The weather can change in an instant."

"But it was only raining on us. People quite close to us were still sitting in bright sunshine. It was as though he'd created our own personal rain cloud."

Susan managed a smile, but was dying a little inside. "Was there anything else?"

"Lots of little things, but nothing major until the one I've already mentioned to you. One day, not long after we were married, the next door neighbour's dog wouldn't stop barking, so Gary turned it into a statue. He hadn't realised I was there. That's when he came clean with me."

"Told you that he was a wizard?"

"That's right."

"What did you say?"

"I laughed of course. Just like everyone laughs at me now. I thought he was off his head. But then he told me about this other place called Candlefield."

"That's where the supernaturals live?"

"Yeah."

"Where exactly is Candlefield?"

"That's just it. Only supernaturals can go there."

"How did Gary travel back and forth between here and there?"

"He used magic, but not all supernaturals can do that. Werewolves and vampires have to travel there by road."

"Did Gary ever try to take you there?"

"No, but he couldn't have even if he'd wanted to. Candlefield doesn't exist to humans. It took me a while to get my head around that idea. Once he'd decided to tell me that he was a wizard, he showed me lots of different magic. He made himself invisible. He levitated. He could pick up things which were really, really heavy. It was unbelievable."

"What about your kids? Did they see any of this?"

"No. Gary didn't want them to know. He said it would be too dangerous."

"What happened once he'd shared his secret with you?"

"We knew we had to keep it quiet because sups aren't allowed to tell humans that they exist. If they do, they're likely to get taken back to Candlefield, and won't be allowed to come to the human world ever again."

"Who takes them back?"

"It's a kind of supernatural police force. They're called Rogue Retrievers. Their job is to find any sups who break the rules in the human world. That's what happened with Gary. Somehow, and to this day I still don't know how, someone found out that Gary had told me he was a wizard. That's why he was taken."

"Did you actually see these Retrievers take him away?"

"No. I was at the shops. When I came back, he'd gone."

"So you don't actually know for sure that it was the retrievers who took him away?"

"Of course I do. Where else would he have gone?"

"People disappear all the time."

"Gary and I had never been happier than just before he disappeared. He didn't walk out, Susan. Somehow they must have found out that he'd told me he was a wizard, so they took him back. I know they did."

Susan and Margie talked for quite some time. Susan wanted to make sure that when she left, Margie felt that she'd been given a full and fair hearing.

"Okay, Margie, I've got everything I need, but you really must leave it with me now. I'm very busy, and I can't have you calling into the office all the time to ask what's happening."

"I won't. I trust you, Susan. I know you're going to look into this."

"I will, but it's probably going to take some time. So you'll have to be patient."

"I understand. All I've ever wanted was for someone to take me seriously." She hugged Susan again. "Thank you so much."

Susan felt bad for deceiving Margie, but what choice did she have? She had to get her off her back.

As she drove down the street, it occurred to Susan that she might as well talk to Margie's two daughters. It would be interesting to get their take on what had happened, and maybe she'd be able to persuade them to talk to their mother, and try to get her to see sense.

She called first at number thirty-two where, according to Margie, Willow lived. A woman answered the door. By her side was a boy no older than seven.

"Can I help you?"

"Hi. My name's Susan Hall. I've just been talking to your mother, and I wondered if I might have a couple of minutes of your time."

"What's it about?"

"It might be better if we spoke inside. It won't take long."

"Okay." Willow led the way inside. "Jason, go and play in your room while Mummy talks to this lady."

"Okay, Mummy." Jason rushed upstairs.

"What's it about? Is Mum all right?"

"Yes. At least, I think so. I work at The Bugle."

"Oh, no." Willow's face dropped. "Don't tell me she's been talking to you about wizards."

"She has, actually. Yeah."

"I was hoping that she'd forgotten about that. She hasn't mentioned it to me for a while, but that's probably because every time she does, I get angry with her."

"I assume you know that your mother thinks your father was taken away by —"

"Supernatural creatures? Yes, I know the whole sorry story. According to her, my father is a wizard, and he was taken away by the Rogue Retrievers to Candlefield where all the supernaturals live. I've heard it a thousand times."

"I take it that you don't believe it."

"Of course I don't. Surely you don't either. Look, I love Mum to bits, but this is getting really annoying. I get that she's upset, and I hate my father for what he's put her through, but the idea that he's gone off to some supernatural land is crazy. I wish Mum would just drop it. I'm worried about the effect it will have on Jason if she starts talking to him about it. He'll have nightmares."

It was quite obvious that Willow thought her mother

had lost the plot entirely. After leaving Willow's house, Susan made her way to number forty-one where Margie's older daughter lived. Rose answered the door at the first knock.

"I just saw you come out of my sister's house."

"Yeah. I've been to your mother's as well."

Susan explained to Rose why she was there, and what her mother and Willow had said.

"I think Willow should try to be a bit more understanding."

"Oh?" Susan had expected Rose to hold similar views to Willow.

"Mum and Dad were really happy together. He would never have walked out on her. I'm sure something's happened to him."

"But you surely don't believe this story about Candlefield?"

"No, of course not. I don't believe in witches and wizards, or things that go bump in the night, but I do think that Dad was taken away against his will by someone."

"And you have no idea by whom or why?"

"None. If you could find out, that would be great."

Chapter 15

Charlie and Dorothy were in the lounge. Neil was in the kitchen. Susan wasn't yet home.

"Neil!" Charlie said. "Will you pass me the biscuit tin?"

"What's up with you, lazybones? Why don't you get off your backside and fetch it?"

"Please, Neil. I'm comfortable. You're coming over here anyway, aren't you?"

"I'm going to make myself a drink first." Neil cast a spell, and the biscuit tin began to float across the room towards Charlie.

Just then, the door opened and Susan walked in. She stared in disbelief at the biscuit tin, which was floating across the room. The other three looked at her in horror. Neil lost focus on the spell, and the tin crashed to the floor, spilling biscuits everywhere.

"What's going on?" Susan turned to Neil.

"Nothing. Everything's normal." He quickly cast the 'forget' spell while Charlie began to pick up the biscuits.

Susan shook her head, seemingly dazed. The 'forget' spell had worked.

"Err—hi, everybody. Sorry, I lost it there for a moment. Hey, where did that bird come from?"

"That's Bob." Neil got in before Dorothy had the chance to answer.

"Bob?" Susan walked over to the cage.

"Stupid name, eh?" Neil laughed.

"There's nothing stupid about his name," Dorothy said. "My mother gave him to me."

"I like canaries." Susan tapped the bars of the cage. "Hello, Bob."

"See!" Dorothy turned to Neil. "Susan likes our new flatmate."

Still a little disoriented from the 'forget' spell, Susan joined the others in the lounge. She deliberately took a seat as far away from Dorothy as she could. She didn't entirely trust her after the finger pricking incident. Sooner or later, they would have to have a talk to clear the air, but she didn't want to do it while the guys were there.

"How was work today, everyone?" Susan said.

"I wasn't in today," Charlie said. "It was my day off, so I went to visit my mum. I usually go and see her about once a week."

"Does she live in Washbridge?"

Charlie hesitated. He hadn't thought this through—he couldn't tell Susan that his mother lived in Candlefield. "No, not in Washbridge, but not far away. The visit was a bit of a disaster."

"Don't you and your mum get on?"

"We get on like a house on fire. We always have. I lost my dad when I was young, and since then Mum and me have been very close."

"What went wrong today?"

"It's my brother, Ralph. He's a teenager, and he's causing quite a few problems."

"All teenagers are like that."

"I know, but Mum's worried he's going to push it too far, and end up in trouble with the—" He stopped himself just in time. He'd almost said Rogue Retrievers. "With the police."

"Why? What's he been up to?"

"I don't really want to get into all that. Mum asked if I'd

have a word with him, but I think I actually did more harm than good. He doesn't want to listen to any adult—not Mum, and definitely not me. We ended up having a stand-up shouting match. Mum had to pull us apart. I didn't hang around after that because I didn't want to make things even worse."

"What about you?" Susan turned to Neil. "How's the fancy dress business?"

"It was my day off, too. I went to see my parents as well."

"Hopefully you had a better time than Charlie."

"Not really. At least Charlie gets on with his mum. That's more than I can say about me and my parents. I've cut down the visits to once a month, but even that's too often."

"Why? What's the problem?"

"Nothing I do is ever good enough for them. I'm one big disappointment in their eyes. They hate that I work here in the—here in Washbridge." He'd almost said 'the human world.' "And they don't like me working in the fancy dress shop."

"What's wrong with the shop?"

"There's nothing wrong with it. I'm perfectly happy there. It's just that they had bigger plans for me."

"What kind of plans?"

"They—err—" Neil had dug himself into a hole. He could hardly tell Susan that they were disappointed because he was only a level three wizard. "They wanted me to study law, but it wasn't for me."

"What about you, Dorothy?" Susan asked.

"I didn't go to work today, either. I should have, but I phoned in sick. I went to see my mum too."

"So, all three of you have family around here?"

"Yeah," Dorothy said. "Not far away."

"Do you get on okay with your mum, Dorothy?"

"Me and Mum get on fine. She misses me though, and the dog really misses me."

"You've got a dog?"

"Yeah, her name's Babs. I can't keep her here, so Mum looks after her. That's why she got me the canary. She also said that she'd like to come over, and paint a portrait of us all, but I told her 'no'."

"Why?" Susan said. "That sounds like a great idea."

"To be honest, she's not that good."

"I'm sure you're being unfair on your mother," Charlie said. "I bet she's brilliant. No one thinks their parents are any good at anything. It would be cool to have a portrait of us all. We could have it up there on the wall."

"Yeah, I'd be up for that," Neil said.

"Never going to happen." Dorothy shook her head.

"What about you?" Neil said to Susan. "How was your day?"

"Mixed really. There's an outside possibility I might have a story based on a suspicious death, but it's early days, and it may not come to anything. And, I spent most of the afternoon with a crazy woman. I told you about her the other day. She reckons her husband is a wizard who's been taken back to the supernatural world."

"I remember you mentioning her," Neil said. "It all sounds a bit weird."

"Weird isn't the word. This woman is one hundred percent certifiable. I figured the only way to put a stop to her pestering me at the office was to go to her house, and give her a full hearing. She showed me photos of her husband, and explained how he had proven to her that he was a wizard. Apparently, he made himself invisible, levitated, and even turned their neighbour's dog into a statue."

"Does she really believe he's a wizard?" Charlie asked.

"She's absolutely convinced of it. According to her, he was taken away by—I can't remember their names—retrievers or something. They supposedly take back any supernaturals who are misbehaving." Susan laughed. "I know, I know. It's completely crazy, but this is what I've had to put up with."

"Did you promise to look into her story?"

"Kind of. I even spoke to her daughters who live on the same street. One of them was rather annoyed that her mother kept going on about the wizard thing. She has a young son, and was worried it might have a bad effect on the child. The other daughter was a bit more understanding. She believes her dad has been taken by someone. She doesn't think he would have just walked out. There may be a story there somewhere—not the supernatural rubbish, obviously. But I may take another look at it from the missing person angle."

"Hey, by the way," Neil said. "Have you seen the rota anywhere?"

"I left it on the breakfast bar." Susan glanced over at the kitchen. "Isn't it there?"

"No." Charlie shook his head. "We've looked everywhere, but we can't find it."

"Oh, well." Susan sighed. "I'd better get changed. I'll catch up with you three later."

She didn't believe the rota had mysteriously disappeared. All the time she'd spent drawing it up had probably been wasted. The three of them had most likely decided they didn't like the idea of her reorganising everything. If that was the case, she would have much preferred that they'd told her to her face.

After Susan had changed, she stayed in her room, and did some research on statistics about missing people. It was surprisingly easy to find. The number of adults who disappeared nationally in the course of a year was quite scary. Where did all of those people go? Then she found a better source, which broke it down, region by region, and even city by city. She searched for Washbridge and checked the number. Then she compared that with several other cities of a similar size. The more she checked, the more intrigued she became. The number of missing adults reported in Washbridge on average per year was three times that of any comparable city. That might simply be because the authorities in Washbridge were more diligent about recording such disappearances. Even so, it definitely merited further investigation.

As soon as Susan had gone into her bedroom, Charlie and Dorothy had turned on Neil.

"What were you thinking?" Charlie said, in a hushed voice. "You can't use magic in the apartment now Susan's here."

"You're an idiot, Neil," Dorothy said. "You could have carried the biscuit tin over here. You didn't need to use magic."

"You two worry too much." Neil waved away their concerns. "I sorted it out, didn't I?"

"Only by casting another spell," Charlie said. "What do you call that spell that makes humans forget?"

"Surprisingly, it's called the 'forget' spell." Neil grinned.

"It's not funny," Dorothy chided him.

"It worked, didn't it? She won't remember the biscuit tin incident."

"You can't use magic when Susan's around," Charlie said. "It's too dangerous."

"Okay. Stop panicking. Anyway, I don't know why you're both having a go at me." He turned to Dorothy. "At least I didn't stab her."

"I did not *stab* her! I just pricked her finger with a needle, that's all."

"You can't do that!" Charlie said. "She's a flatmate."

"Okay, okay. No drinking the human's blood. I get it."

Dorothy excused herself. Once inside her bedroom, she knelt down, reached under her bed, and pulled out a sheet of paper, which she folded into the shape of an aeroplane. Then, she threw it out of the open window.

"Bye-bye rota."

Chapter 16

Susan had managed to track down Chris Briggs' brother, Simon; he worked in an insurance office in Washbridge city centre. After a little persuasion, he had agreed to speak to her there during his lunch break.

"Hi, I'm Susan Hall."

"Simon. Shall we go through here?"

Susan followed him to a small room at the back.

"You said you wanted to talk about Chris? Why are The Bugle interested in him?"

"We like to follow up all—err—unusual deaths. It's just routine." Susan knew it was a weak excuse, but it had been the best she could come up with.

"He killed himself. That's all there is to it."

"I'm sure you're right, but still, if you could just answer a few questions, I'd be grateful. Did you have much contact with your brother?"

"No." He shuffled in his chair. "I realise that makes me sound callous, but Chris caused the family a lot of problems—he was always drunk or high. To tell you the truth, when Dad threw him out, I was pleased to see him go."

"What about jobs? Did he ever have one?"

"He got a job straight out of school in the local pharmacy—just helping out in the back. He only lasted there for six months before he got sacked. We never did find out why, but I would bet my life he'd been stealing drugs."

"Did you see him often after your father threw him out?"

"Oh yes, I saw him. I could hardly miss him. He was

always hanging around town—usually drunk or high, or both, but I hadn't spoken to him in years."

"What about friends? Did he have any?"

"Back in the day, yeah. There were four of them who always used to knock around together. I reckon it was them who first got Chris into the drugs."

"Do you remember their names?"

"Let me think. There was Richy—Richard Price. And Alan Charlton. And then of course there was Robert Marks—you'll have heard of him."

Susan shook her head.

"You're a reporter, and you don't know who Robert Marks is?"

"I've only just moved back to Washbridge. I've been in London for several years."

"He's standing for election as MP for Washbridge. His ugly mug is never out of the papers."

The whole discussion lasted no more than fifteen minutes. It was obvious that Simon had long since cut all ties with his brother, and neither knew nor cared about what had happened to him.

When she got back to the office, Susan checked the archives for articles on Robert Marks. There was no shortage of them to be found. A wealthy, self-made business man, who was currently on the Washbridge council, he had recently announced his intention to stand for Parliament. The latest article was a picture of Marks dressed in swimming trunks, as he prepared to swim the first ever length in the recently opened swimming baths.

She tried to contact Marks, but was out of luck because although she'd managed to find his contact details, every phone number she had for him proved to be a dead end. Either there was no reply or she got one of his many assistants who would do no more than offer to take her name and number, and pass them on to Marks. Needless to say, none of her calls were returned.

Undeterred, she decided to visit the pharmacy where Chris Briggs had once worked. As far as she could ascertain, that had been the only job he'd ever had. This too was a long shot because it was many years ago, and there was a good chance that the business would have changed hands since then.

The exterior of Presto Pharmacy looked as though it hadn't seen a coat of paint for over a decade. The sign was in bad repair with the letters 'M' and 'Y' hanging at an awkward angle. The shop was empty except for the bespectacled man behind the counter.

"Yes, madam?" He sounded bored.

"My name is Susan Hall. I work for The Bugle."

"I guess someone has to."

She ignored the jibe. "Are you the owner?"

"I am. Is there a problem? If it's about the nappy promotion—that was just a misunderstanding."

"It isn't. I wanted to ask you about a young man who worked here several years ago. Ten years ago, to be precise."

"You're out of luck, then. I only bought the business six years ago."

"Would you happen to know the name of the person who owned this business ten years ago?"

"I would, but it won't do you any good."

"Why's that?"

"How old are you, young lady?"

"Twenty-six."

"Did you live in Washbridge ten years ago?"

"Yes."

"Then you should remember the Crab Tattoo murder."

"Sorry?"

"The owner of this business was murdered. The case was big news at the time."

It still didn't ring any bells with Susan, but then at sixteen years of age, she had paid very little attention to the local news. She'd been far more interested in music, clothes and boys.

After leaving the pharmacy, she used her phone to research the Crab Tattoo murder case. The articles made rather harrowing reading. The owner of the pharmacy had been hit over the head with a chair. He'd stumbled forward and fallen onto a glass display case, which had shattered—glass from the case had severed an artery. His assailant had left the man to die. Before he did, the pharmacy owner had managed to write the words 'crab tattoo' in his own blood. The police believed he may have disturbed a thief, but despite several appeals they were never able to find anyone with a crab tattoo. The police had also found what they believed to be the murderer's fingerprints on the chair used in the assault, but there was no match on their databases. The case remained open to that day.

Susan made a phone call to Simon Briggs.

"Hi, it's Susan Hall, again. I'm sorry to trouble you."

"That's okay."

"You mentioned that Chris worked in a pharmacy. I've just been reading up about the Crab Tattoo murder case. Did the police talk to Chris about that?"

"Yeah. They questioned him. It wasn't really a surprise because he'd been fired from there not long before, and was known to have a drug problem. They asked him a few questions, and took his fingerprints, but he didn't hear any more about it."

"Okay, thanks."

***

"Charlie!" Greta called through the microphone.

"Is everything okay?" Charlie made his way over to the cupboard.

"Look what we found." She pointed to a crumpled sheet of paper next to the thimbles.

"What is it?"

"Take a closer look."

Charlie picked up the paper, and straightened it out. It was Susan's rota. "Where did you find this?"

"It was on the pavement below the window. When we were out there yesterday, we saw something sailing through the air, so we followed it down to the ground. It took both of us to carry it back up here. It was very heavy, but we managed it. Do you think someone has lost it?"

"No, I don't think so. I think someone has been very naughty."

He could see that the paper had been folded into an aeroplane. The only other bedroom on the same side of the building was Dorothy's. She must have thrown it out of her window. He couldn't help but laugh.

Just then, someone knocked on the door, and stepped inside. It was Susan. "I hope you don't mind me coming in. I just wanted to—" She stared at the paper in his hand.

"What's that, Charlie?"

"What's what?" He put his hands behind his back.

"That!" She pointed. "Behind your back."

"This? It's—err—a plane. It's sort of a hobby of mine."

"Can I see it?" She held out her hand.

"This one isn't very good. I could make you a much better one."

"Please, I'd like to see that one." She insisted.

He reluctantly handed it over.

"Sorry," he mumbled. "I didn't realise it was your rota."

She handed back the crumpled plane. "If you didn't like the idea of a rota, I wish you'd just said so."

"No, Susan, it's not what you think."

At that moment, Neil came into Charlie's bedroom. "Guys, we've got a visitor. You're both needed out here."

Susan turned and followed Neil.

"I'm going to kill Dorothy," Charlie said under his breath.

Bunty was laughing her head off.

***

Dorothy was absolutely shattered. It had been a quiet day at the bookshop, but sometimes they were the worst. She'd been so bored that she'd almost fallen asleep. Her plan was to go straight to her room, lie down, and have a short nap, but when she stepped into the apartment, she was horrified by the sight that greeted her. Susan, Charlie, and Neil were all talking to her mother. Worse still, Dolly had already erected her easel. On it was a blank canvas.

"Mum? What are you doing here?"

"I told you I was going to come over and paint a

portrait of you and your flatmates." Dolly had a huge smile on her face.

"But, Mum, I said we didn't want our portrait painting."

"Yes we do," Neil said. "I think it'll be great."

"Yeah, me too." Charlie nodded. "We could have it on the wall over there."

"I quite like the idea," Susan said.

Dorothy knew it was pointless to argue. She was outnumbered three to one. If she insisted that her mother left, they would all think she was cruel and heartless. But she knew the truth; her mother couldn't paint for toffee. There was nothing Dorothy could do, but join the others. Charlie and Neil took the armchairs, while Susan and Dorothy sat on the sofa.

Dolly put on her smock, grabbed a paintbrush, and began to paint. Dorothy was dreading the outcome. She'd seen so many of her mother's paintings, and they were all the same—absolutely hopeless. What would her flatmates think when they realised that her mum was a fraud?

As was always the case when Dolly painted a picture, it didn't take long. After only an hour, she announced, "Okay, everyone. It's finished. You can all take a look."

Dorothy was the first off the sofa. She hurried behind the easel, and cringed when she saw the finished product. There was what looked vaguely like a sofa, and maybe two armchairs. On them were matchstick figures which bore no resemblance to any of her flatmates. Dorothy was worried that the others would make some snide comments or, worse still, laugh at it.

"That's fantastic, Mum. It's one of your best. It's just so post-modern. Like Charlie said, we'll hang it over there."

By now, the other three were standing behind Dorothy. Neil sniggered, but soon stopped when Dorothy kicked his shin. Charlie had to stifle a chuckle. Susan just looked confused.

"I'm glad you all like it. I must get back now." Dolly tidied away her paints and packed up her easel. "I have to take Babs for a walk. I'll see you soon, Dorothy."

Dorothy saw her mum out, and then turned around to find the others staring at her, puzzled.

"What was that all about?" Neil said.

"You two make me sick," she said to Charlie and Neil. "How could you laugh at Mum like that?"

"But look at it." Neil pointed at the picture. "It looks like a three-year-old did it."

"Be quiet, Neil."

"It isn't very good," Charlie said.

"I quite like it," Susan said. "I agree with you, Dorothy. It's very post-modern. Very now."

Dorothy was taken aback by Susan's reaction to the painting, but she needn't think that was going to win her over.

Chapter 17

The next morning, Susan was on her way to The Bugle's offices when someone called her name. It was the reporter from The Chips. It took her a moment to remember his name. Tom Wallace, that was it.

"I was hoping I'd bump into you," he said. "I've got something I want to show you." He produced a newspaper from behind his back. "This is our first copy. What do you think?"

The first thing she noticed was the name of the publication: 'In The Wash.'

"Is that the best name you could come up with?" Susan laughed. "It's terrible."

"Actually, I agree. I didn't have any say in that. Still, it's a great newspaper. Have you seen the headline?"

Susan glanced again at the paper. The headline read 'The Last Post.' She skimmed it quickly. It accused her newspaper of not supporting the residents of Washbridge, and being too focused on sensationalist stories. In The Wash promised to step into the void, and to fight the important issues on their behalf. All in all, it was a real hatchet job on The Bugle.

"Here," Susan pushed the newspaper back into his hand. "You can keep it. I'm not impressed."

"There's still a job for you at In The Wash," Wallace said. "It's not too late, but you'll need to make your mind up quickly."

"I've already told you that I'm not interested. I'm not worried by competition. I thrive on it."

"Fair enough." He shrugged. "If you won't take the job, will you at least have a drink with me?"

"No, thanks."

"Why not? Do you have a boyfriend?"

"That's none of your business." She turned and walked away, which would have been a lot easier to do if he hadn't been so very good looking. But she wasn't about to fraternise with the opposition.

Before she went back into the office, she made a phone call to Dreams.

"Hi, Susan. How are you settling in?"

"Okay. Early days, but so far so good."

"I see there's a new newspaper in town."

"Yeah. Their first issue's out today."

"Is that going to be a problem for you?"

"It will make life a bit more interesting, but I like a challenge. Anyway, I rang to see if you fancied going out tonight? Jess will probably be up for it too."

"I can't. I'm sorry. I've already got something on tonight. I could meet you straight after work for a quick drink though, if you like?"

"Yeah, okay. Where do you want to meet?"

"How about Downtown?"

"Down town where?"

"That's the name of the bar. It used to be The Crown."

"Oh, right. Yeah. What time?"

"How about five-thirty?"

"Okay. See you then. I won't bother telling Jess. The three of us can have a proper night out another time."

"I hear you've landed yourself a major scoop." Dougal Andrews caught Susan as soon as she walked into the office.

"What scoop would that be, Dougal?"

"A little bird told me that you went to Margie's house yesterday. What's your headline going to be? 'My Husband the Wizard'?"

"I've no intention of running a story about wizards, witches, or any other make-believe creatures for that matter. I just thought I should do Margie the courtesy of hearing her out. Something you should have done a long time ago."

"You thought you'd shut her up, more like. I've got news for you, Suzy, it won't work. Once the word gets out that you've got a sympathetic ear, every nutjob in Washbridge will be headed your way."

"Thanks, Dougal, but when I need your advice, I'll know it's time to quit."

She'd no sooner taken a seat at her desk than Flynn beckoned her into his office.

"I assume you've seen this." He had a copy of In The Wash on his desk.

"Yeah, just now. I bumped into one of their reporters, Tom Wallace. He was the one who wrote this article."

"Have you read it?"

"I've only glanced at it, but it doesn't make great reading."

"The sad thing is that most of it's true. The Bugle have failed Washbridge residents, which is why you and I are here. But this is going to make our job a lot more difficult. If we don't turn things around quickly, it may be too late. Are you working on anything promising at the moment?"

"A couple of things, but it's early days. I can't really say much about them yet."

"Okay," Flynn sighed. "I know you'll do your best, but

the sooner the better. We need headlines, and we need them yesterday."

Susan went back to her desk. It was obvious that Flynn was under pressure, which meant that she was too. Chris Briggs' death may or may not yield a big story; it was too early to tell. Then there was always the extortion story which Manic had offered her. She was tempted to give him a call, but decided against it. Susan didn't want her first ever story in The Bugle to come from some unsavoury character she'd met in the basement car park. She had to come up with her own.

***

"Hey, Susan," Stella said. "Do you fancy going for a coffee?"

Susan glanced at her watch. She hadn't even realised it was lunchtime.

"Sure, why not. Where do you want to go? Coffee Triangle again?"

"Definitely not. It's Gong Day. It'll be unbearable in there."

They decided to go to Aroma.

"I've started to look for a job again," Stella said, once they had their drinks.

"Really? Why?"

"Now that other newspaper has opened, I think the writing's on the wall. No disrespect to you, Susan. I know that you'll do a good job, but I think The Bugle's days may be numbered. I want to get out of the newspaper business altogether. I've applied to lots of different places: estate agents, accountants, in fact anywhere they need an admin assistant or receptionist."

"You have to do what's best for you, Stella, but I'm still hopeful that The Bugle will ride out this storm."

"Flynn looks worried."

"He does, and I can't blame him. If things do go pear-shaped, then he'll be back on the job market like the rest of us. I'll probably have to go back to London, which between you and me, is not something I want to do right now."

"I'm surprised you moved up here. It must be very boring compared to London."

"True, but London can get pretty tedious at times. It's so busy everywhere, and the commute can be awful."

After they'd finished their drinks, they headed back to the office. They were almost there when Susan heard someone call her name. She turned around to find Tony standing across the road.

"Stella, you carry on. I'll just be a few minutes."

Susan waited for Tony to come over.

Before they'd both left for university, Susan had thought Tony was the one. They'd both promised to remain faithful while they were apart, but that hadn't worked out even though Susan had kept her part of the bargain.

"Hi." He looked a little embarrassed.

"Tony," she said, coldly.

"I didn't know you were back."

"There's no reason you would." She wasn't going to make this easy for him.

"How long have you been here?"

"A few days."

"Look, Susan." He stared at his feet. "I'm really sorry

about, you know, what happened between us."

"That's in the past." She waved it away as though it was nothing. In truth, at the time, it had broken her heart. But she would never let him know that.

"I didn't plan for it to happen, you know."

"I see. So you accidentally fell into bed with her, did you? Anyway, why are we even discussing this? It's history now."

"I just wanted you to know that I never meant to hurt you."

"And now you've told me."

"You probably heard," he continued. "I'm no longer with Lisa."

"Jess told me."

"I don't think Jess likes me. Whenever I've seen her, she's been very cold towards me. In fact, she gave me a right telling off once."

"Well, that's Jess for you." Susan grinned. "She always did speak her mind."

"I don't suppose you'd like to go for a drink sometime, would you?"

"Goodbye, Tony." And with that, Susan turned and walked away.

***

After work, Susan made her way to Downtown. It was a small bar, which was a little too pretentious for Susan's liking. Dreams was waiting inside for her.

"It's great to see you again, Susan."

Dreams had already ordered a tonic water for herself. "What do you want to drink?"

"Just an orange juice for me."

"How's the job going?" Dreams asked when they'd found a quiet corner table.

"So far so good. There's a lot of pressure to come up with the big stories, and so far, there's precious little to be had. Anyway, don't let's talk about me. What about you? What have you been up to?"

"Just the usual."

"I assume you're still working in the shop?"

"Of course."

After leaving school, Dreams had gone to work for the family business; a small gift and card shop on the outskirts of Washbridge. She'd never been the ambitious type.

"Are you still with Ryan?" Susan kept hoping that Dreams would come to her senses, and dump that sorry excuse for a man.

"Of course. Why wouldn't I be?"

"No reason. You just haven't mentioned him for a while."

"I don't mention him to you because I know you don't like him."

"That's not true."

"Liar. I've never understood why, though."

Susan shrugged. "You're not engaged yet, then?"

"Ryan says there's no hurry, and I guess he's right."

Susan decided it was best to get off the subject of Ryan. "Jess wants the three of us to have a night out some time."

"I'm not sure Ryan would approve."

"Come on, Dreams. You're entitled to a night out with your friends every now and then."

"I guess so, but I couldn't have made it tonight. I've got

something on."

"Anything exciting?"

"You'd only laugh if I told you."

"Now you've got me intrigued."

"If you must know, I'm going to a meeting of PAW."

"Paw? What's that? Some kind of animal charity?"

"It's P-A-W. Paranormal Activity Watch."

"Since when were you interested in the paranormal?"

"I've always believed that we share this world with fairies, goblins, witches, and all manner of supernatural creatures."

"Are you serious?"

"Deadly. I've been going to PAW every week now for nearly two years. I wouldn't expect you to be interested in stuff like that."

"I might be, as it happens."

"You're just taking the mickey now."

"No, I'm serious. I don't suppose I could come with you tonight, could I?"

"Not if you're going to write an article, and make us all look stupid."

"You know me better than that. I'm your friend."

"You're my friend, but you're also a journalist, and I know what journalists are like. The story comes first."

"I would never do that to you. You helped me get this job. I'm not going to stab you in the back, am I?"

"I'm still not sure it would be a good idea."

"What harm can it do?"

Dreams checked her watch. "I have to be there in thirty minutes. Are you sure you want to come?"

"Definitely."

"Okay, but you have to promise you won't write a story

about PAW?"

"I promise." Susan crossed her heart.

They each took their own car. Susan followed Dreams. PAW held its meetings in an old church hall on the west side of Washbridge Park. Susan had no idea what to expect, but in the back of her mind she had a picture of lots of Margies, each with their own conspiracy theory. She fully expected whoever was in charge of PAW to be the mad professor type.

She couldn't have been any more wrong.

There were about twenty people in the church hall when they arrived. The majority were women. There were people of all ages, from a teenager to an old lady who looked to be in her eighties.

"Everyone. This is Susan," Dreams announced. "She's an old friend of mine who's just moved back here from London."

There was a chorus of greetings. Susan smiled, said 'hi,' and then took a seat next to Dreams.

A few minutes later, a young man walked to the front of the room. He was not at all the mad professor type she'd been expecting. He was young—probably only a couple of years older than Susan. He was very smartly dressed in a suit which made him look like a banker. And, he was really good looking.

"Evening, everyone." He looked around the room. "I see we have a new face."

"This is Susan," Dreams said. "She's come with me tonight. I hope that's okay, Greg."

"Of course. I'm Greg Lewis, Susan. You're more than welcome. Hopefully you'll find it interesting, and become a regular visitor."

One woman reported that she'd seen a ghost, who was now apparently a regular visitor to her house. Another spoke of fairies that she insisted lived at the bottom of her garden. Susan said nothing because she was under strict instructions from Dreams not to pass comment.

After the meeting had finished, and the others started to drift away, Susan managed to get hold of the guy who'd been running the meeting.

"Excuse me. Could I ask you a few questions?"

"Of course. Fire away."

"I'll be honest with you, I'm a reporter."

His expression changed immediately.

"I'm not here to get a story or to make fun of you. I promise."

"Okay, but we've had a few problems with the press before. We're an easy target, as you can imagine."

"I'm sure. Could you tell me what prompted you to form PAW?"

"I've always had an interest in the paranormal. And the fact is, there are more reports of paranormal activity in Washbridge than in any other town or city in the UK."

"You mean in towns or cities of a comparable size?"

"No. I mean *any* town or city in the UK. There are three times as many reports of paranormal activity in Washbridge than anywhere else in the UK."

"That's incredible. Could that be because you're so active here?"

"I'm sure that has some effect on the numbers, but it doesn't explain such a high volume of reports. Anyway, Susan, what brings you here today?"

"A woman called Margie came to see me. She's

apparently been badgering the reporters at The Bugle for some considerable time. According to Margie, her husband was a wizard. He was supposedly snatched away from his family, and taken back to another land — somewhere the paranormals live. Apparently, the reason he was taken back was because he'd told his wife he was a wizard. I realise this must all sound crazy."

"Not necessarily," Greg said. "You should speak to Mary Dole."

"Is she here tonight?"

"No. She came to a couple of meetings, several months ago, but then left the group. I haven't seen her since. She told exactly the same story. That her husband was a wizard, and that he'd been taken back to another land. In fact, she even had a name for it. Candle — err — "

"Candlefield?" Susan prompted.

"That was it. Candlefield."

Dreams had arranged to meet her boyfriend, Ryan, after the PAW meeting had finished for the evening.

"What did you think of it, Susan?" she asked, as she was about to leave.

"It wasn't what I expected."

"How do you mean? Because they didn't all turn out to be nutters?"

"I suppose so." She couldn't fault the sincerity of everyone who'd been at the meeting, and she had been particularly impressed by Greg Lewis. He seemed to be in no doubt that paranormal creatures existed. Susan could never buy into that, but she did think there might be the germ of a story there somewhere.

More than anything else, she was fascinated by what

Greg had told her about Mary Dole, the woman who had apparently told a story similar to Margie's. Susan fully intended to follow that up at some later date. Maybe what she was actually witnessing was a case of mass delusion.

Chapter 18

When he arrived home from work, Neil bumped into Craig, another wizard, who lived on the floor below them.

"How's it going, Craig?"

"Great, thanks. I'm having a party this weekend, and I'm inviting everyone in the building. Are you up for it?"

"What do you think?" Neil grinned. "Have you ever known me to turn down a party? Will there be plenty of women there?"

"Yeah, and plenty of drink, too. I'm planning on pushing the boat out. What about your flatmates?"

"I'm sure they'll be up for it. Why don't you come up and ask them yourself?"

"Okay." He followed Neil upstairs.

Charlie, Dorothy and Susan were all sitting in the lounge. Neil led the way inside; Craig was a few steps behind him.

"Everybody! Craig's having a party this weekend! He wants to know if you're all up for it."

"Count me in!" Charlie said.

"Sure." Dorothy nodded.

"I'd love to come," Susan said. "Thanks very much for the invite. It will give me a chance to get to know everyone."

When Neil turned around, he noticed the worried expression on Craig's face.

"Neil, can I speak to you outside?" Craig said in a hushed voice.

Neil followed him back out.

"Why didn't you tell me?" Craig said, once they were outside.

"Tell you what?"

"That your new flatmate is a human."

"It never occurred to me."

"I can't have a human at the party."

"Why not? Susan's okay."

"The party is strictly sups only. How are we meant to let our hair down, and enjoy ourselves, if we've got to look over our shoulder all the time to make sure the human isn't spying on us?"

"She's not a spy. She's a —" Neil hesitated.

"A what?"

"Actually, she works for The Bugle. She's an investigative reporter."

"Great!" Craig rolled his eyes. "A human *and* an investigative reporter? Does it get any worse than that?"

"Sorry."

"What on earth possessed you three to take her on as a flatmate?"

"We didn't have any say in it. The landlord said we'd been dragging our heels. He was the one who told her she could have the place. There was nothing we could do about it."

"Well, she can't come to the party."

"What am I supposed to tell her? She thinks she's been invited."

"Tell her what you like. Just don't bring her."

Craig went back downstairs, leaving Neil wondering what he was going to do about Susan. He re-joined the others in the lounge.

Dorothy held up a copy of a newspaper. It was the first edition of In The Wash. "This doesn't look very good for The Bugle, does it?"

Susan was determined not to let her concern show. Instead, she tried to remain upbeat. "I'm not scared of a little competition. Remember, I learned my trade in London. There are any number of newspapers in the capital. And besides, if the first issue is anything to go by, I don't think we have much to worry about."

"You must be a bit worried," Charlie said.

"Obviously, it's going to make life more difficult, but it's nothing we can't overcome. If I was worried, I would have jumped ship to the other paper when I had the chance."

"They offered you a job?" Neil said.

"Yeah. Their chief investigative reporter has asked me to join them twice now."

"And you turned him down?"

"Of course I did. Anyway, enough newspaper talk. I met up with an old friend of mine, Dreams, after work."

"Dreams?" Charlie looked puzzled. "Is that a name?"

"Her name's actually Caroline Day, but we've always called her Dreams. She took me to a meeting of PAW— Paranormal Activity Watch."

"The what?" Neil looked horrified.

"You heard right. Paranormal Activity Watch. Dreams goes there every week. She wasn't too keen on the idea of me tagging along because she thought I was after a story. Anyway, I managed to persuade her to let me go with her, and it turned out to be very interesting—not at all what I expected."

"Isn't it full of nutjobs?" Dorothy said.

"Surprisingly, no—most of the people there seemed quite normal. They all take it very seriously. I've also learned a few interesting facts about Washbridge."

"Such as?" Charlie asked.

"Did you know that more adults go missing here than in any other town or city of comparable size?"

That information hardly came as a surprise to the other three. They already knew that a lot of sups were taken back to Candlefield by the Rogue Retrievers.

"And that's not all," Susan continued. "I was talking to Greg Lewis. He's the guy who runs PAW. He's young, smart, and very down to earth. Not at all what I'd expected. He told me there are more reports of paranormal activity in Washbridge than in any other city in the UK, regardless of size. And not just a few more — there are three times as many as the nearest one."

"But surely all this paranormal stuff is nonsense," Dorothy said.

"I suggested to Greg that the reason for the high numbers being reported was because of the presence of PAW, but according to him, the figures are too high to be explained away like that."

"Sounds to me like you're buying into this rubbish," Neil said.

"Of course not. But there may still be a story there somewhere, if only from the missing person angle. Anyway, I'm going to follow it up. Do you remember I mentioned the woman who insists that her husband was a wizard, and that he was taken away by something called a rogue retriever? Well, now Greg has given me the name of another woman who told him exactly the same story. She said that her husband had been taken back to Candleton — no, that's not it — Candle — err — "

"Candlefield," Charlie said.

The other two glared at him.

"You've heard of it, Charlie?"

"No—err—yes. Someone must have mentioned it to me. I can't remember who though."

Susan talked for another fifteen minutes about PAW while the other three listened in silence—too stunned to say anything. Then she stood up. "I need to nip to the shop. I'm out of orange juice. Does anyone else need anything while I'm there?"

None of them did.

As soon as she was out of the door, Neil and Dorothy turned on Charlie.

"Candlefield?" Dorothy almost exploded. "Candlefield? What were you thinking?"

"I'm sorry. I don't know what came over me. I'm really sorry."

"Now she's been to that stupid Paranormal Activity Watch, she's probably going to pursue this further," Dorothy said. "We have to stop her talking to the other woman whose husband was taken back to Candlefield."

"How are we meant to do that?" Neil said.

"I don't know, but there must be something we can do."

"There isn't. We don't even know who the woman is. The only thing we can do is make sure we don't give her any more ammunition. And that means not mentioning Candlefield again, Charlie."

"Yeah, I've already said I'm sorry. Anyway, you can't talk—you were using magic in front of her—remember the biscuit tin?"

"You're right," Neil conceded. "I won't do it again."

"And you, Dorothy," Charlie said. "You can't keep trying to drink her blood."

"I don't intend to. That was just a one-off."

"We've got another problem," Neil said. "Craig doesn't want Susan at the party."

"But he invited everyone."

"Yes, but I'd omitted to tell him that Susan was a human. He assumed that we'd got another sup as a flatmate."

"We've got to get her to move out," Dorothy said. "It's too dangerous having her living here."

"How are we meant to do that?"

"There's only one way. We have to get Socky to scare her away."

"But she's already been in her bedroom for several days now. It's freezing cold in there. And then there's the sound of him clomping around with his wooden leg on the floor. None of that seems to have scared her so far."

"Socky is just going to have to up his game." Dorothy turned to Neil. "And you're going to have to persuade him to do it."

"Me? Why me?"

"Who else? Charlie and I can sense his presence, but you're the only one who can see him, and have a proper conversation with him. You've got to make him see that having a human living in the apartment is dangerous for everyone—including him. What would happen if she took it upon herself to bring in a Ghost Hunter? You've got to make Socky realise that this could affect him too."

"That's all well and good," Neil said. "But you know what Socky's like. He's very set in his ways, and he doesn't like being told what to do."

"In that case, you'd better use all your powers of persuasion. The ones you use on all of your lady friends."

"You're right." Neil suddenly looked quite smug. "I can be quite persuasive when I want to be."

"Go on then. There's no time like the present." Dorothy ushered him towards the bedroom. "Before Susan gets back."

"Socky, are you there, Socky?" Neil called.

The ghost appeared. "It's Tobias." He sighed. "How many more times must I tell you?"

"Sorry, Tobias. Look, we've got a bit of a problem with the woman who's staying in your room."

"In my office, you mean?"

"We need to get rid of her."

"Why don't you just throw her out?"

"That won't work. She's been given the room by the landlord. So as long as she keeps paying the rent, we can't get her out."

"What has the world come to?" Tobias tutted. "I never used to have these problems in my day. If I wanted someone out of one of my properties, I just showed them the door."

"Things have changed since then."

"Not for the better, apparently."

"We can't have a human living here."

"A human? What do you mean? We're all humans."

"That's not true. You're a ghost, and the three of us—well, we're not human."

"You're not bringing up this wizard nonsense again, are you?"

"I know it's hard for you to get your head around, Tobias, but it's true. Anyway, take it from me, having the human in this apartment is bad news for everybody. She may take it upon herself to bring in a Ghost Hunter."

That made Tobias look up. "What is that, exactly?"

"They're people who specialise in ridding places of ghosts. If she brought one in, you could end up back in Ghost Town permanently."

"That horrible place? It's full of ghosts."

"That is rather the point, Socky — err — Tobias."

"I won't be thrown out of my own office."

"That's why you have to scare her away."

"That's proving to be easier said than done. If she could see me, I'm sure I could send her running. But I can't do that unless she allows me to attach myself to her, and I doubt that is going to happen."

"You could make the room even colder, and make even more noise."

"I'll try, but it takes a lot of energy. You have no idea."

"Do your best, Tobias. The sooner we get her out of here, the better for all of us."

Just then, the door to the bedroom opened. Neil spun around to find Susan standing there. She'd seen him talking to the wall — or at least that's how it had appeared to her.

"Neil, why are you in my room?"

"I just — err — I came to — err — look at the heating to see if I could sort it out, but it seems to be working okay."

"But it's still so cold in here."

"I know. It must be the direction the room faces. I think it faces north."

That sounded like nonsense to Susan. "Who were you talking to when I came in?"

"No one." Neil gulped. "I often talk to myself when I'm doing something. I was just saying, '*Well, there's nothing to be done in here, Neil*'." With that, he quickly reversed out of the room.

Susan was beginning to have serious doubts about her flatmates.

That night, Socky did everything he could to scare Susan. The temperature in the room dropped dramatically — it was even colder than usual. She had to pull all the covers over her just to keep warm. He spent all night walking up and down, his wooden leg clunking on the floor as he went. Every time Susan fell asleep, he would clunk his leg even louder to wake her up. But in the end, tiredness overtook her, and she fell into a deep sleep from which not even Socky could wake her.

Chapter 19

When Susan woke up the next morning, her room was still freezing. And yet, when she checked the radiator, it was warm, and seemed to be working fine, just as Neil had said. So how come the room was so cold? She checked the window for any gaps, but the seal looked fine. A thought crept into her mind, one that she'd had a few times before, but had tried to ignore: What if the room was haunted? She'd read somewhere that the presence of a ghost could cause the temperature of a room to drop dramatically.

The other housemates were eating breakfast.

"Hey, guys. Look, I know this might sound a little cuckoo, but do you think there might be a ghost in my room?"

"A ghost?" Dorothy did her best to sound surprised by the question.

"I wouldn't normally suggest anything so crazy, but I can't understand why it's so cold in there. The radiator is working, and there's no draught coming through the window, and yet last night it was freezing. And then there's the noise. It's as though somebody's walking across the room back and forth, all night long."

"It is a very old building," Charlie said. "I suppose it could be haunted."

"Greg, the man who runs PAW seems a decent kind of a guy. I might ask if he has any experience with ghosts. Maybe I can get him to come over and take a look at my room."

The three other flatmates were stunned into silence.

"Anyway," Susan said, "I'd better get off to work."

As soon as she'd left, Neil turned to the others. "So much for your brilliant idea. What are we going to do now? What if this Greg guy is a sensitive?"

Sensitives were humans who had a closer connection to the paranormal world than the average person. They could sense the presence of not only ghosts, but of other sups too.

"We can't afford to let him come here," Dorothy said.

"There's no way of stopping him," Neil said. "We'll just have to make sure that he doesn't find anything. The three of us can't be here when he comes, in case he can sense that we're sups."

"That's all well and good," Dorothy said. "But what about Socky? He'll definitely sense Socky is here, and if he does, he's likely to launch a full-scale investigation of the whole building. You have to persuade that stupid ghost to vacate the room when this guy comes over."

Neil led the way into Susan's bedroom. "Tobias!" he called. The other two flatmates gave him a puzzled look. "What? That's his name. I have to call him that or he gets upset. Tobias!"

Socky appeared, but was visible only to Neil.

"What is it now? I need to get some sleep. I've been up all night."

"You were supposed to scare the human away."

"I did my best. I spent all night walking around this room. Why do you think I'm so tired?"

"Well, you failed miserably. Not only is she not leaving, but she's going to bring in a sensitive."

"A what?"

"A sensitive. They can sense the presence of ghosts."

"How very interesting."

"No, it's not, trust me. If he senses you're here, he'll bring a Ghost Hunter in, and you'll be banished to Ghost Town forever."

"I can't possibly have that."

"Exactly. So you'll have to go back to Ghost Town when this guy comes."

"But it's awful there."

"Better to go back there for just one day than forever."

"I suppose so." Socky sighed. "But it's most inconvenient. When is he coming?"

"I don't know, but as soon as I do, I'll give you the nod, and then you'd better make yourself scarce."

***

Susan phoned Greg.

"Hi, Susan. How are you?"

"Fine, thanks. Am I right in assuming that you believe in ghosts?"

"Of course. Why do you ask?"

"I feel silly even mentioning this, but the room I've just moved into is incredibly cold, and yet the heating is working fine. And then there's the noise."

"What kind of noise?"

"It's almost as though someone is walking back and forth across the floor. It went on all last night. I barely slept."

"Have you actually seen anything?"

"No. It's just the cold and the noise. Look, it doesn't matter. It was silly of me to mention it."

"No, wait! Where is it you live?"

"It's what used to be the old sock factory on Colbourn

Drive. Do you know it?"

"Yes. Leave it with me, and I'll see what I can find out about the history of that building."

"Thanks, Greg."

***

Susan had tried several times to get hold of Robert Marks, but she'd had no joy. She was beginning to think it would have been easier to get an audience with the Queen than to get to talk to Marks. So instead, she'd decided to try and trace the other two friends of Chris Briggs: Richard Price and Alan Charlton.

Working at The Bugle, she had plenty of resources at her fingertips, which made it relatively easy to track people. What she found shocked her. Both men had moved away from Washbridge some years earlier. But that wasn't the only thing they had in common. They were both dead. The details were sketchy, but from what she could make out, Richard Price, who had moved to Swindon, had died in a road accident about four years earlier. Two years later, Alan Charlton, who had moved to Sheffield, had died in a climbing accident.

Susan understood that coincidences happened, but her reporter's instincts sensed there was something decidedly fishy going on. She'd been able to contact the widows of both men, and they had both agreed to talk to her.

First stop: Swindon.

Kirsty Price, Richard Price's widow, met her at the door.

"Thank you so much for agreeing to see me."

"No problem. Do come in. I was rather surprised when you phoned about Richard. It's been a while since I've talked about him with anyone."

Kirsty made them both a drink, and they settled down in the lounge.

"I came across Richard's name when I was looking into the death of Chris Briggs, who I believe was a friend of your late husband?"

"The name doesn't ring a bell."

"According to Chris Briggs' brother, there were four of them who used to hang out together, but I am going back ten years."

"That might explain why I don't know him. I didn't meet Richard until eight years ago."

"Do you remember your husband mentioning an Alan Charlton or Robert Marks?"

"No, sorry, but then Richard rarely talked about the life he led before we got together. Whenever I asked him about it, he always shrugged off the question. He said everything that happened before we met was unimportant." She managed a smile, but had tears welling up in her eyes.

"When did you move to Swindon?"

"We met at uni, and both moved here straight after we'd got our degrees. I landed a job here first, and Richard got one six months later. What exactly happened to this Chris Briggs? Why are you investigating his death?"

"He supposedly jumped from the multi-storey car park in Washbridge."

"I assume you don't think it was suicide otherwise you wouldn't be investigating?"

"The person who brought the story to me didn't. I have an open-mind. I believe your husband died in a car accident."

"He died in a car *crash*. Whether or not it was an accident, no one really knows."

"How so?"

"He was travelling to Scotland on business. The car left the road, went down an embankment, and hit a tree." Kirsty hesitated, and took a deep breath.

"I'm sorry to upset you."

"It's okay. I don't mind talking about it. No mechanical faults were found, and there was no evidence that Richard had braked before the car left the road."

"Were there any witnesses?"

"No. The crash happened on a quiet road, late at night. The wreckage wasn't spotted until the next morning."

"Is there any other reason why you suspect the crash may not have been an accident?"

"The unexplained head injury, and the blood."

"Can you elaborate?"

"According to the pathologist, one of the head injuries *might* not have been consistent with those suffered as a result of the crash. It was to the back of his head."

"Might not?"

"The pathologist said he couldn't be one hundred per cent sure that the injury didn't result from the crash, but he thought it unlikely."

"And the blood?"

"They found traces of someone else's blood in the car."

"Had he been travelling with someone?"

"Not to the best of my knowledge."

"Could he have picked up a hitchhiker?"

"I doubt it. Richard never stopped for them."

"What conclusion did the police come to?"

"None really. They checked the blood against their DNA database, but there was no match. They appealed for witnesses in case anyone had seen Richard with someone else, but no one came forward. In the end, an open verdict was returned at the inquest."

"What do you think happened?"

"I prefer to think it was an accident. The alternative is too horrible to even contemplate."

Susan was more sceptical, but didn't air her thoughts.

She grabbed lunch at the motorway services: sandwiches which tasted like cardboard followed by lukewarm, weak coffee.

Next stop: Sheffield.

Alan Charlton's widow, Marie, didn't answer the door when Susan knocked. She tried again, but still no joy. Great! If she'd travelled all that way for nothing, she wouldn't be best pleased. Susan rang the number she'd contacted Marie on earlier.

A woman answered on the first ring. "Hello?"

"Hi there. This is Susan Hall. I arranged to come and see you. I'm at your door, but there's—"

"Sorry. I'm in the garden around the back. Hold on. I'll be with you in two ticks."

Moments later, the door opened.

"Sorry about that. I'm fighting a losing battle with the bindweed. Do come in."

Marie showed Susan into the dining room, and then went to wash her hands.

"Tea?" she called from the kitchen.

"Yes, please. Milk and one sugar."

"You said you wanted to speak to me about Alan?"

Marie passed Susan her tea, and then joined her at the table.

"I'm investigating the death of Chris Briggs, who I believe was a friend—"

"Chris Briggs? I remember him. He used to knock around with Alan—him and a couple of other guys. Now, what were their names? Richy and Bob, I think."

"Richard Price and Robert Marks?"

"Yes, that's them. You say Chris died? The last I heard, he was living rough."

"That's right, he was. He apparently jumped from the multi-storey car park in Washbridge."

"Suicide? That's terrible. But in that case, why are you investigating it?"

"There's a possibility it might not have been. At least according to someone who knew him quite recently."

"I see. How can I help?"

"I wondered if I might ask you about your husband's death?"

"Alan died in a climbing accident. Climbing was his passion." She managed a weak smile. "I hated it, as you might imagine. I always told him that something would go wrong one day, but he insisted it was safe. I've never been more sorry to be right about anything."

"I read that it happened in the Peak District."

"That's right. It's right on our doorstep. Alan often used to climb there."

"Was he with someone when it happened?"

"That's the weird thing. Alan always said that anyone who climbed solo must be crazy, and yet on the day he died, he'd been climbing alone, apparently."

"Do you have any idea why?"

"No. The strange thing is that two other climbers told the police they'd seen him with someone earlier in the day, but he was alone when he fell. His body was found by other climbers."

"Had he made arrangements to climb with someone?"

"He climbed with lots of different people. He didn't used to bother telling me who he was going with. To be honest, I wasn't interested. I just wanted him to pack it in altogether."

"I take it no one came forward afterwards?"

"No."

"Was there an enquiry?"

"Just the inquest. They said it was accidental death, and I guess they're right. Alan should never have climbed alone."

They talked for almost an hour in total. Marie had many memories of the group of four friends, but nothing that would help Susan in her investigation into Chris Briggs' death.

"Okay. Thanks for seeing me. I hope I haven't upset you too much."

"Not at all."

Susan started for the door.

"Wait! I think I have a photograph of Alan with the other three guys. You can borrow it if you want to."

"Yes, please."

"Just hold on. I'll go and get it."

Marie returned ten minutes later, holding a creased photograph.

"Sorry. It took a while to find. It was in an old album at the back of the wardrobe. They'd been playing football when this was taken."

Susan studied the photograph of four fresh-faced young men dressed in football shirts and shorts. They were all laughing at something.

"That's Alan." Marie pointed to the man second from the left. That's Richy, that's Bob and that's Chris. It's scary to think that two of them are dead now."

"Three." Susan corrected her.

Marie looked puzzled.

"Didn't you know? Richard Price died in a car crash four years ago."

***

Susan was on her way back to Washbridge when her phone rang. She pulled into a layby to take the call. It was Greg.

"Susan, I've done some research on the sock factory, and found something interesting. There were two unusual deaths reported there in the early part of last century. The first was a woman named Isadora Braithwaite who fell to her death from a top floor window. The other was a man named Tobias Fotheringham who was the factory owner at the time. The reports are rather vague, but it would appear that he was in the factory by himself one night— there's a suggestion that he may have been drunk. Anyway, he somehow fell into heavy machinery. I'm sorry, but this is rather gruesome. It tore his leg off, and he died from blood loss. They found him the next morning. He'd somehow managed to crawl back to his office, apparently."

Susan shuddered at the thought. "Do you think it's possible that I'm being haunted by the ghost of one of those two? Isadora or—what did you say his name was?"

"Tobias. It's certainly a possibility."

"Is there any chance that you could come over to the apartment, and take a look at my room to see if you can sense anything?"

"I'd be glad to. I can come over now, if you like?"

"I'm just on my way back to Washbridge. I should be home by about six o'clock, if that's any good?"

"That's fine. I'll call around then."

Chapter 20

"Bunty? Greta? Are you there?"

Charlie was standing next to the cupboard looking through the magnifying glass at the thimbles. Greta poked her head out of her living room window. Bunty was upstairs in her bedroom.

"Could you do me a favour?" he said.

"Of course," Greta said immediately.

"What now?" Bunty groaned. "I was just about to take a nap."

"Come on, Bunty," Greta said. "Charlie is always helping us out, and he lets us live here for free."

"I suppose so. What is it?"

"You know we've got a new flatmate?"

"Yes, she's very pretty," Greta said.

"She's nothing special." Bunty shrugged.

"The thing is, she's convinced there's a ghost in her bedroom."

"That's because there *is* a ghost in her bedroom." Bunty shuddered. "It's that horrible sock man with the peg leg. He gives me the creeps."

"Can you actually see him?" Charlie sounded surprised.

"Of course. Starlight fairies have always been able to see ghosts. Didn't you know?"

"I had no idea."

"He should be prosecuted for being that ugly," Bunty said.

"Bunty!" Greta turned on her friend. "That's just cruel."

"Anyway," Charlie continued. "Susan's just phoned to say that she's invited the guy from Paranormal Activity Watch to come over at six o'clock. Neil, Dorothy and me are going to make ourselves scarce — it's too risky for us to be here when he comes. If I leave my bedroom door open, would you two listen in on their conversation to see if there's anything we need to worry about?"

"We'll be glad to," Greta said.

***

As soon as Susan had phoned to tell them that Greg was coming over, Neil told Socky that he had to vacate the premises immediately. The ghost moaned and groaned, but he knew which side his bread was buttered, so made his way back to Ghost Town.

When Susan arrived home, she found she had the apartment to herself. Or at least, she thought she did. Unbeknown to her, two tiny fairies were running surveillance for Charlie.

"Greg, thanks for coming over," Susan greeted him at the door.

"This is a great place you've got here. It's so big."

"Yeah, but then there are four of us living here."

"Five, if you count the ghost." Greg grinned. "Where are your flatmates?"

"I don't know. They must have all gone out."

"Maybe they're paranormal creatures, and are scared I'll suss them out?"

"That must be it." Susan laughed. "More likely, they all think I'm crazy. They've lived here for ages, and they don't seem at all concerned there might be a ghost."

"So which is your room?"

"This way."

As soon as she opened the door to her bedroom, she

realised the temperature was the same as the rest of the apartment. Greg followed her inside.

"I thought you said it was cold in here?"

"It's usually freezing, but it seems okay now." She felt more than a little embarrassed.

"Not to worry. Why don't I set up my stuff to see what I can find?"

Greg had brought a case full of equipment. It took him about fifteen minutes to set everything up on the cupboard next to the bed. They sat there for an hour while Greg watched the dials on the meters, and listened through his headphones.

Eventually, he pulled off the headphones. "I'm not getting anything at all, Susan. Not a thing."

"Maybe it's gone. The temperature seems to be back to normal. And usually, if I'm in here for any length of time, I can hear a knocking sound as though someone is walking across the room."

"I'm certainly not sensing anything."

"I'm sorry I've wasted your time, Greg."

"Not at all. Even though I believe in the paranormal, I know that one's imagination can conjure up all kinds of things."

"I guess so." Susan was beginning to doubt herself now. Had she imagined the temperature drop, and the knocking sound?

As Greg made his way out, he hesitated. "You did say the sounds and cold were just in your bedroom, didn't you?"

"Yes, why?"

"There's just something about this room."

Susan looked around. "What?"

"I don't know. Maybe it's nothing. I just sense there's been some kind of paranormal activity in here. Maybe I should take some readings in this room?"

"No, it's okay. The others could be back any minute. I don't want them to think I've gone totally crazy."

"Are you sure?"

"Certain, but thanks again for coming over."

"My pleasure."

***

After Greg had left, Susan took out the photograph that Marie had given to her. Three out of the four men on it were now dead. One suspicious suicide, one suspicious car crash, and a climbing accident that also raised a few questions. She was about to put it back into her handbag when she noticed something on Alan Charlton's leg. It was so small, Susan could barely make it out, so she nipped through to Charlie's bedroom, and put it under the magnifying glass. It was a tattoo — a very small, simple tattoo. A circle with the letter 'A' inside it. Then she noticed that Chris Briggs had a similar tattoo on his leg. His was a circle with the letter 'C' inside it. She checked the other two men, but they were standing side-on to the camera, so she couldn't see if they also had tattoos.

She made a call to Kirsty Price.

"Kirsty, it's Susan Hall."

"Hello again."

"This might sound like a daft question, but did Richard have any tattoos?"

"Just one. On his leg. A circle with the letter 'R' inside it. I asked him about it numerous times, but he just said he'd had it done when he was drunk."

"Did he mention if his friends had similar tattoos?"

"No, but like I said, he didn't like to talk about his past."

"Okay, thanks, Kirsty."

Susan's heart was racing. She had a hunch, and if she was right, this could turn out to be the big story she'd been hoping for. She went through to her bedroom, took out her laptop, and brought up the recent article on Robert Marks. The one where he'd been opening the new swimming baths.

"Yes!" She punched the air. There on Robert Marks' leg was a very faint scar in the shape of a circle. It was the kind of scar left when a tattoo has been removed. Next, she searched for any articles about Marks on or around the dates of the deaths of Robert Price and Alan Charlton. Forty minutes later, she had found what she was looking for.

***

When the other flatmates got back, Charlie went straight into his bedroom, making sure to close the door behind him.

"Greta? Bunty?" He peered through the magnifying glass.

"Hi, Charlie." Greta greeted him with a smile.

"I was just about to wash my hair," Bunty complained.

"Did you hear what Susan and the guy from Paranormal Activity Watch had to say?"

"We did," Greta said. "They—"

"There's good news and bad news," Bunty interrupted.

"The good news is he didn't find any trace of ghost activity in her bedroom."

"Thank goodness. What's the bad news?"

"He said he thought he sensed paranormal activity in the main room."

"Oh no. What's he going to do?"

"Nothing. He wanted to carry out more tests, but Susan said she didn't want you lot to think she was crazy."

***

That night, at about midnight, Susan woke up. The room was freezing cold. Moments later, she heard the familiar knocking sound. The ghost, or whatever it was, was back. Susan wondered how come it had disappeared when Greg had come over? It was as if it had known he was coming.

The next morning, when it was time to get up, Susan was still half asleep. She hadn't slept very well at all.

"I don't know what's going on," she said to the others who were in the kitchen. "When Greg came over yesterday, the temperature in my room was fine, and there were no knocking sounds. But then, last night, it started again. I have to get to the bottom of this. I'm going to ask him to come back and do more tests."

The other three housemates were horrified.

"You don't need to do that, Susan," Neil said. "I actually prefer a cooler room. I don't sleep well if it's too warm. Why don't I swap rooms with you?"

"Really? It seems an awful imposition."

"Not at all. I'd be glad to do it. You'd be doing me a favour."

"Well, okay, if you're sure."

"Absolutely. We can swap over tonight."

"Great. Thanks."

After Susan had left for work, Neil turned to the others. "I hope you realise what a sacrifice I'm making for you two."

"It's your own fault," Dorothy said. "You were the one who invited Socky here in the first place."

"At least now I know what to get you for Christmas." Charlie grinned. "You're going to need some thermal pyjamas."

***

Later that day, Charlie was assisting one of his female clients with a rowing machine when his phone rang.

"Mum? Is everything okay?"

"No, it isn't, Charlie. Ralph's gone to Washbridge again, with one of his friends. I overheard them talking. I'm sure they're going to turn werewolf, and scare humans. I'm worried about what might happen. Do you think you could bring him back home?"

"He could be anywhere, Mum. I wouldn't know where to start."

"I heard them mention Washbridge Park. Do you know it?"

"Yes. It's nearly time for me to knock off for the day, so I'll get over there."

"You have to find him, Charlie." His mother sounded desperate. "Before he does something stupid."

"Don't worry, Mum. Everything will be okay."

The light was already fading. Washbridge Park covered

an extensive area. If he was going to find Ralph, Charlie would have to search in a logical manner. He started at the north end of the park, and worked his way slowly down, checking every area of bushes and trees.

There were very few people around, just a few dog walkers. The park was an eerie place after dark. There were only a few street lights, and several of those weren't working. Charlie spotted a man walking by himself in the distance. He was the first person he'd seen who didn't have a dog with him. If Ralph and his friend were in the park, they wouldn't pick on someone with a dog because the barking might attract attention.

Charlie hurried over. The man had taken the path that led through a tunnel of bushes. Sure enough, as Charlie got closer, he spotted movement in the undergrowth. The next thing he knew, two werewolves jumped out. The man stumbled and fell. Charlie could see the look of terror on his face, which was illuminated by a single street lamp. He recognised Ralph immediately, even though his brother had turned full werewolf. Ralph's friend was much smaller. Both wolves were approaching the human who was lying on the ground, shaking with fear. Having scared the man, it was possible they planned to leave it there, but Charlie couldn't take that risk. What if they dragged him into the bushes? What if they killed him?

Charlie turned werewolf. He was far bigger and stronger than his younger brother and his friend. He batted the smaller wolf across the head, and sent it flying back into the bushes. Then he grabbed his brother, shook him, and pushed him backwards.

"Get back to Candlefield, both of you! Now!" he growled.

Neither of them was a match for Charlie. Although Ralph was prepared to give his brother verbal when they were in human form, he wasn't going to cross Charlie now they were both wolves.

The two young wolves hesitated for a moment, then turned and ran. As they did, Charlie saw them change back into human form. They would be on their way back to Candlefield in no time.

The human was still lying on the ground, shaking with fear. He was staring at Charlie, who was even more scary than the two wolves who had first attacked him.

Charlie turned back into human form, found his phone, and called Neil.

"It's Charlie. I'm in Washbridge Park. It's urgent. Can you get over here now?"

"What's going on?"

"No time to explain. It's a matter of life and death. Get over here now, please. I'm near the west gate."

"Okay. I'll be there in a few minutes."

Sure enough, minutes later, Neil came rushing into the park. Charlie shouted from within the bushes. "Neil, I'm over here."

The human was still lying on the ground, too scared to move.

"What's going on?" Neil glanced at the stricken man.

"I need you to cast that spell which will make him forget everything that's happened in the last few minutes."

Neil checked there was no one around. "Okay, you go home. I'll see to this."

Thirty minutes later, Neil was back at the apartment.

"Everything okay?" Charlie asked him.

"Yeah, it's fine. He won't remember anything. What happened, anyway?"

"It was Ralph. He came over with one of his friends. They'd already scared the human half to death, and I was worried they might do something worse, so I had to step in."

"You don't think they would have killed him, do you?"

"I don't know. I wasn't going to wait around to find out. Thanks again, Neil."

Chapter 21

It was Saturday morning. Dorothy, Charlie, and Neil were in the kitchen. Susan had gone out long before any of them were even out of bed.

"How are we going to stop Susan going to the party, tonight?" Neil said. "Craig won't let her in his apartment."

"This is your fault, Neil." Dorothy unwrapped her granola bar. "Why didn't you mention that Susan was a human when he told you about the party?"

"It never occurred to me."

"We have to think of some way to stop her," Charlie said. "Can't you cast some sort of spell, Neil?"

"That won't work. I can make a human forget something that's just happened, but there isn't a spell that will make them forget an event that's yet to take place."

"In that case, there's only one thing we can do." Charlie took a bite of toast. "We'll have to tell Susan that the party's been cancelled."

"How is that going to work?" Dorothy said. "She'll hear the noise from up here. You know what Craig's parties are like. They're not exactly quiet affairs."

"We have to get her out of here, and keep her away until the party's finished."

"You mean miss the party?" Neil looked horrified. "But I love Craig's parties."

"There are more important things at stake right now," Dorothy said.

"Hang on a minute," Charlie interrupted. "You could be right. But it can't be me or Neil who asks her out. She'll think we're trying to hit on her, and turn us down. It has to be you, Dorothy."

"Me? Go out with Susan?"

"It's the only way," Neil agreed. "If you ask her out, she'll think you're trying to make amends because, let's be honest, you haven't exactly welcomed her with open arms, have you?"

"I can't spend all evening with that human."

"You'll have to," Charlie said. "It's the only way. Tell Susan the party's been cancelled, but that you fancy a night out. I'm sure she'll go out with you because she wants to be your friend."

"And what are you and Neil going to do while I have to listen to that human babble on all night long?"

"We'll go to the party, of course."

"I thought you might."

"Come on Dorothy," Neil said. "You have to take one for the team, like I did when I swapped bedrooms."

"That's easy for you to say. You're going to be enjoying yourselves while I have to put up with Susan human-face." She sighed. "Go on then, I don't suppose I have any choice."

***

"I'm looking forward to the party tonight," Susan said when she arrived back at the apartment. She'd spent the morning choosing a new dress.

"I've got bad news about the party." Dorothy was the only other flatmate still in the apartment.

"Why? What's wrong?"

"It's been cancelled," Dorothy lied.

"What? I've just bought a new dress on the strength of

that party. Why?"

"Apparently, Craig hasn't been feeling well. He sent word with Charlie that he's had to cancel."

"Well that's a bummer." Susan sat down on the sofa. "I was looking forward to meeting all the other people who live in the building."

"It would be a shame to waste your new dress. Why don't we have a night out?"

"You mean the four of us?"

"Nah, we don't want the guys to come—they'll cramp our style. I thought we could have a girls' night out, just you and me. It would give us the chance to get to know one another." Dorothy was putting maximum effort into this. The last thing she wanted to do was have a night out with Susan, but she had to sound convincing.

"That sounds like a great idea."

***

It just wasn't fair, Dorothy reflected as she and Susan set out on their night out. The guys still got to go to Craig's party, and that guy knew how to throw a party. She'd been to several, and they'd all been brilliant. Instead, she had to go out with Susan, and what was worse, she had to pretend like she wanted to be there.

"Where are we going?" Susan asked.

"I thought we could start at Bar Twenty-Four, and then perhaps move on to a club afterwards."

"We're going to a nightclub as well?" Susan sounded surprised.

"Yeah, why not? We may as well make a night of it." She knew she had to keep Susan away from the apartment until the party was over.

Dorothy went straight on the vodkas; Susan had the same.

"Are you ready for another?" Dorothy asked.

Susan had barely taken a sip of hers. "Err — no, not yet."

"Another vodka." Dorothy shouted to the barman.

Before long, the drink began to take effect, and she and Susan were chatting away like long lost friends.

"What's it like living in London?" Dorothy's eyes were already a little glazed.

"I liked it. There's tons to do. That's the thing, once you've lived in London, everywhere else seems a bit quiet."

"Did you have a boyfriend down there?"

"Not really. Nothing serious."

"Who did you live with?"

"I shared an apartment with one other girl called Yvonne."

"I still don't understand why you came back here. There must have been other reporter jobs in London." Dorothy took another swig of her vodka.

"There were always jobs cropping up, but there's a lot of competition for them too. I would've got something eventually, but it just so happened that the job at The Bugle came up. It was a challenge, and a lot more responsibility than I would have got at a big London newspaper. Even if I only stay here for a couple of years, it'll look good on my CV. What about you? Do you like working at the bookshop?"

"For now, but I'm not sure how long I'm going to stick around here, though."

"Where else would you go?"

"Err—I don't know." Dorothy had to check herself. She'd almost said she might go back to Candlefield. "I might try my luck in London. There are plenty of jobs down there, aren't there?"

"Yeah, but everything is very expensive. Even the smallest apartment costs a fortune. You'd probably have to live a long way out and travel in. If you don't mind a lengthy commute, it could be okay."

"I might do that." Dorothy glanced at her watch. "Come on, let's go to a club. I feel like dancing."

They moved on to a nightclub called Surrender. It cost an arm and a leg to get in, and was absolutely packed. The music was a bit loud for Susan's taste, but Dorothy seemed to love it.

"Let's get some shots," Dorothy said.

"I'm not sure."

"Come on. Let your hair down." Dorothy bought shots for them both. Moments later, they were on the dance floor. Dorothy had lost all her inhibitions, and was really getting into the groove. Susan tried to keep pace. A few guys hovered around, but none of them made a move.

When it was time to go home, Dorothy was definitely the worse for wear, and Susan wasn't far behind her.

"It's been really good tonight." Dorothy hiccupped. "You're not so bad after all."

"Thanks. You're okay yourself."

"We'd better get a taxi."

"Let me pay for it," Susan insisted. "You bought most of the drinks."

As Susan lay in bed, the room began to spin a little.

She'd been disappointed that the party had been cancelled, but at least it had given her the opportunity to bond with Dorothy. Maybe now, they would have a better relationship.

***

The next morning when Susan emerged from her room, she spotted Dorothy disappearing out of the door. Susan gave chase because she wanted to thank her for the previous night.

"How was your night out, Susan?" Charlie called after her.

"Great, thanks," she said, as she hurried out. "I've got a bit of a headache this morning, but it was worth it. I want to catch Dorothy."

When she stepped out onto the landing, she spotted Dorothy heading not downstairs, but up to the floor above. Susan was about to follow when she heard another voice. It was Dorothy's friend, Tilly. "Dorothy, where were you last night? You missed a great party. Everybody was there. Craig was asking after you."

Susan couldn't believe her ears. The party hadn't been cancelled at all. Dorothy had lied to her. What was it with that woman?

***

Susan's phone rang; caller ID told her that it was her mother's landline. Although her mother had a mobile phone, she rarely used it.

"Hi, Mum."

"Hello, Susan." Her father's voice took her completely by surprise. It had never occurred to her for one minute it might be him calling.

"Oh? Hello, Dad. How are you?"

"I'm very well, thank you. I know you and I have had our differences, but your mother told me that you're back in Washbridge. I wonder if we could meet for lunch, just the two of us, to see if we can clear the air?"

"Yeah, of course. I'd like that."

"Can you make today?"

"Yes, but there's somewhere I need to be at three."

"How about one o'clock, then? Do you know The Sparrow?"

"Yes."

"Okay, I'll see you there at one."

"See you then."

Susan was still staring at the phone long after the call had ended. When she'd decided to return to Washbridge, she'd known that sooner or later she would have to face her father, but she had hoped it would be later. She'd expected their first conversation would be heated, but he'd seemed almost conciliatory. That wasn't like him at all. She could only assume that her mother must have told him he had to get it sorted. Susan wanted that too. She didn't want this atmosphere hanging over them.

Chapter 22

Susan and her father both arrived at The Sparrow at precisely one o'clock. He was full of smiles, and gave her a big hug. It seemed almost too good to be true.

"I've booked a table over there in the corner." He led the way inside, and once seated, he ordered the drinks. Susan had a soda water; he had a beer. The meal, although very simple, was perfectly acceptable. All through it, they made polite conversation. They talked about her brothers, her mother, and all manner of things, but neither of them mentioned the subject that had torn them apart. Just when Susan was beginning to relax, her father changed tack.

"I was talking to an old acquaintance of mine, Bill Ruthers. I don't think you know him."

Susan shook her head. Her father had so many friends, it was hard to keep track.

"He now runs a lifestyle magazine called 'The Bridge.' You might have seen it?"

"No, I don't think so."

"It's only available in Washbridge and the surrounding area, but it does quite well. It's very well thought of."

"That's nice." The warning bells were starting to ring in Susan's head.

"Anyway, I was speaking to him over lunch the other day, and he told me that they were looking for a full-time editor. It's a good opportunity, and very well-paid. I mentioned your name, and told him you were back in the area after working in London. He seemed very interested. I said you'd give him a call."

Susan could feel the heat rising in her cheeks, but she didn't want to lose her temper. She had to stay calm. "I have no interest in working at a lifestyle magazine. I'd die of boredom. I'm an investigative reporter, Dad. That's what I've been doing for the last three years."

Her father's expression changed. The smile he'd worn all the way through lunch melted away, and she could sense the anger in him. "Don't you realise what the press did to me, Susan? They tarnished my reputation."

"I know, and it was unforgivable. The story they ran was a complete fabrication — they admitted as much."

"Yes, but the damage was already done by then. Don't you see that? That's the problem. They can say what they like, attack who they like, and even if it's proven to be a complete pack of lies, the mud still sticks. People always believe that there's no smoke without fire."

"I know. But that was one bad apple. One bad journalist. That's not what I'm about. The stories that I bring in will be based on hard work and investigation. I take pride in my work."

"And doesn't it matter to you what the press did to me?"

"Of course it does, but this is my career."

"I've had enough of this." He stood up. "I promised your mother I would try. I even managed to find you an another job, but still you throw it in my face." He took out his wallet, and put two twenty-pound notes on the table. "That should cover it." And with that, he left.

"That went well." Susan sighed.

***

Robert Marks was due to attend the opening of the new extension to the Washbridge Tennis Club at three o'clock.

"Are you a member?" A fussy little woman put up a hand to halt Susan.

"I'm press." She flashed her card.

"Oh? Okay." The woman let her through.

The room was surprisingly crowded. On the stage were two women, and one man who Susan immediately recognised as Robert Marks.

"Quiet, please!" The tall woman on the stage clinked her glass with a spoon. "Everyone, please make sure you have a glass of champagne, and then take a seat."

Susan took a glass even though she had no intention of drinking.

"We are honoured to have councillor Robert Marks with us today. As many of you will already know, Mr Marks is hoping to be elected as MP for Washbridge. Please give him a warm welcome."

The crowd duly obliged. Not to be too conspicuous, Susan managed a rather half-hearted clap. What followed was a terminally boring speech by a man who was more interested in winning votes for his upcoming election campaign than in the new extension to the tennis club.

"So, ladies and gentlemen." Marks raised his glass. "Please join me in a toast to the new extension."

Everyone joined in the toast.

Susan's gaze never left the glass in Marks' hand. Moments later he was in among the crowd, mingling and offering platitudes to the electorate. Susan was still watching him like a hawk. As soon as he put his glass down, she picked it up using a tissue, and placed it in a plastic bag, which she slid into her handbag.

Once she was back at her car, she made a call to her brother, Ray, and asked him to meet her at Aroma the following day.

She'd no sooner finished on the call to her brother than her phone rang. It was Yvonne, her old flatmate from London.

"Yvonne?"

"Susan, thank goodness."

"What's the matter? Are you okay?"

"Yeah. Eddie came around here last night."

Susan's heart sank. "What did he want?"

"What do you think? He wanted to know where you were."

"It's just as well I didn't tell you, then. He didn't do anything stupid, did he?"

"No. He'd been drinking. I could smell it on him. He just shouted at me, and said I must know where you were."

"What did you tell him?"

"The truth, that I don't know."

"Did he say what he wanted?"

"What do you think? He wants to talk to you. I don't think he's accepted it's over yet."

"I'm sorry to have put you in this position, Yvonne."

"It's okay. I'm not worried about Eddie, but I am worried about you. He was angrier than I've ever seen him. He said he would find you wherever you were. Will he be able to, Susan?"

"No," she said, with as much confidence as she could muster. But what would happen if Eddie did find her? She didn't want to think about it.

***

"Hey, Neil!" Charlie shouted. "Have you seen Pretty?"

Neil shook his head. "No, can't say I have."

"What about you, Dorothy?"

"No, and I don't want to." Dorothy glared at him. "I've told you, Charlie, we can't have that smelly cat in here. If Redman finds out, we'll all get thrown out."

"Susan, have you seen the cat?"

"Not since my first day here."

"I'm a bit worried." Charlie frowned. "It's been a few days since she's been around. That's not like Pretty. Are you sure you haven't seen her, Dorothy?"

"Why are you asking *me* again?"

"Because I know you. If you had seen her, you would have chased her off."

"You're right, I would, but I haven't. Good riddance, anyway."

Pretty wasn't Charlie's cat, but that didn't stop him worrying. What if she'd been hit by a car or something? What if she was lying injured somewhere? He couldn't settle, so he went out and began to walk the streets.

"Pretty, Pretty!" He earned himself a few strange looks from men and women alike. "Pretty, where are you, Pretty?"

Charlie didn't care about the looks he got; he was only interested in making sure that Pretty was all right. He would never forgive himself if anything had happened to her.

An hour later, he was almost half a mile from the apartment. Surely, she wouldn't have strayed so far? Charlie had no idea where Pretty actually lived. If he had known, he would have called on them just to make sure she was okay. She normally turned up at his door every day, but he hadn't seen her for a few days now. He wondered if Dorothy had chased her away. Charlie liked Dorothy, but he hated the way she treated Pretty.

He was on the verge of giving up when he just happened to glance down an alley between a chemist's shop and a bookmaker. And there, sitting on top of a bin, was Pretty. She was looking up at something — maybe a bird.

"Pretty!" The cat looked around, meowed, jumped off the bin, and came rushing towards him. Charlie scooped her up into his arms. "I've been worried about you." He stroked her, and she purred loudly. "Come on, let's go back to the apartment, and I'll give you some food. I don't care what the others say. Where have you been?" The cat kneaded his chest.

When they were on the landing, outside the apartment, Charlie put Pretty onto the floor, and then opened the door. The cat shot inside. At that precise moment, Dorothy opened the door to the birdcage, and Bob, the canary, came flying out. Pretty saw it immediately, and went charging across the room. She leapt onto the sofa, and hurled herself at Bob. But the canary was too quick for the cat.

"What have you done, Charlie?" Dorothy screamed. "Get that cat out of here before it kills Bob!"

"Come here, Pretty!" Charlie rushed into the room.

The cat was in no mood to listen; she was too focussed on her prey. She leapt from sofa to armchair and back again. She ran over to the lounge and then back to the kitchen. The bird seemed to be toying with the cat.

Eventually, Charlie managed to grab Pretty, and Dorothy got hold of Bob, and put him back in his cage.

"What were you thinking, Charlie?" Dorothy yelled.

"I just brought her in to give her some food. She hasn't been fed for several days."

"Of course she has. She probably gets fed at four or five different places. Look at her, she hasn't gone short of food. She nearly killed Bob!"

"You shouldn't have let him out. You promised you'd keep him in his cage."

"I waited until everyone was out. I thought it would do him good to stretch his wings. Just get that smelly cat out of here!"

"No. I'm going to feed her first." He went to the cupboard, and brought out one of the tins of cat food.

"Why are you keeping cat food in the apartment?"

"If you can have a canary, I can have a cat." He put the bowl of food on the floor for Pretty, and then went to the fridge to get her some milk.

Thirty minutes later, Pretty had had her fill of food and milk, so Charlie took her back outside.

"I see you found the cat." Susan met Charlie on the street, and followed him back upstairs.

"Yeah. Thank goodness."

"Dorothy, can I have a word, please?" Susan had been biding her time, but she knew she had to get this sorted once and for all.

"Sure."

"Not here. Can we talk in my bedroom?"

"I guess." Dorothy followed her.

"Why did you lie to me about the party?"

"How do you mean?"

"I know it wasn't cancelled. I heard you talking to your friend from upstairs. Why did you lie to me?"

"I—err—I thought a night out would give us a chance to bond. It did, didn't it?"

"Well, yes, but—"

"I'm sorry, I shouldn't have lied, but that Craig is always hitting on me. You know how it is. I didn't really want to go to the party. Do you forgive me?"

"Err—yes, I suppose so."

"Thanks." Dorothy made a quick exit.

Susan was even more confused than ever. Dorothy was proving to be something of an enigma.

Chapter 23

Ray arrived at Aroma at nine o'clock on Monday morning, as arranged.

"This had better be important, Susan." He didn't look happy.

"I need a favour."

He laughed. "Why would I do you a favour after the way you've treated Dad?"

"Can we leave Dad out of this? If my hunch is right, this will be a feather in your cap too."

"What hunch? What are you talking about?"

She took out the plastic bag containing the champagne glass, and put it onto the table. "I need you to check the fingerprints on this against those you have on file for the Crab Tattoo murder."

"The what?"

"It was about ten years ago. A pharmacist was murdered, but before he died he managed to write 'crab tattoo' in his blood."

"What does that have to do with this glass?"

"Just do as I ask. I'm sure you'll find they're a match."

"Whose fingerprints are on the glass?"

"I can't tell you that."

"Do you seriously expect me to do this without even telling me whose fingerprints they are?"

"I'll tell you if they match. If they do, and I'm confident they will, you'll have a man guilty of not one, but possibly four murders."

"Four? Who are the other three victims?"

"I'll tell you when you confirm there's a match."

Ray thought about it for a while. "Okay. I'll do it, but if

they're not a match, and you've been messing me around—"

"Just do it, Ray. You'll thank me."

After her brother had left, she made a call to Mary Dole, the woman Greg had mentioned to her when she'd been at the PAW meeting. The woman who had told a similar story to that of Margie. She got through on the first attempt.

"Hi. My name is Susan Hall. I'm a journalist with The Bugle."

"Sorry. I don't want to speak to you." The woman hung up—not a great start.

Not to be deterred, Susan tried again. "Please don't hang up. Can I just have a quick word?"

"What about?"

"I believe your husband disappeared."

"Yes, he did. What's that got to do with The Bugle?"

"Perhaps nothing, but I'd like to talk to you about the circumstances of his disappearance. I understand they were rather unusual."

"Sorry. I don't want to talk about it." The line went dead again.

She was getting nowhere fast, so Susan decided to approach it from a different angle. She called Greg.

"Greg, it's Susan."

"Hello again. Still having problems with the ghost?"

"No. That's all sorted now. One of the other flatmates has swapped rooms with me, but thanks for your help, anyway. When I came to the meeting with Dreams—err—I mean Caroline, you mentioned the woman who had talked about her husband being a wizard."

"Mary Dole, yes. What about her?"

"I managed to trace her, but she won't speak to me. Is there any chance you could contact her on my behalf, and see if you can persuade her to talk to me? Explain to her that I'm not trying to make her look silly. I'm just trying to corroborate what Margie has already told me."

Greg was a little hesitant at first, but in the end, agreed to try. "I'll give her a call, but if she says no, then no it is."

"Okay."

An hour later, he called back.

"I've spoken to Mary, and she's agreed to speak to you tomorrow."

"That's great. Thanks very much."

"Just a minute. There are two conditions."

"What are they?"

"Firstly, the conversation must be strictly off the record."

"Okay. That's fine."

"And secondly, that I'm with you when you talk to her."

"Sure, no problem."

***

The next day, Susan met up with Greg, and together they went to visit Mary Dole at her house.

"Hello, Greg," Mary greeted him with a smile.

"This is Susan Hall." Greg stepped aside.

Mary's welcoming smile evaporated when she turned to Susan.

"Come through to the lounge. Have a seat."

Once they were all seated, Mary said, "Before we start, I

told Greg that this has to be off the record, otherwise I'm not doing it."

"I understand." Susan nodded. "I'm curious though why you're so reluctant to talk about the experience?"

"When Gordon disappeared, I was desperate to talk to someone who might understand. The police weren't interested, so I thought I might get a better hearing from PAW. And to be fair, I did. But I soon realised that most people outside of PAW don't want to know the truth. Whenever I told someone what had happened, the reaction was always the same. They looked at me as though I was completely insane. I was worried that if I continued to tell my story, I'd be in danger of losing my friends, and maybe even my job, so I decided it was better to keep it to myself."

"What exactly did happen to your husband?" Susan asked.

"Gordon and I had only been married for three years. We were both in our late thirties when we met. He was different from any other man I'd ever known. He was kind and very funny, but I always felt as though he was hiding something. Nothing sinister, but he seemed to have secrets. And then, over a period of time, I noticed a few things that just didn't seem right. He'd do little things when he thought I wasn't looking; things that seemed almost fantastical."

"What kind of things?" Susan was eager to get more detail.

"There was one occasion when we went into a homeware shop in Washbridge, and I saw a chest of drawers which I really liked. When we got out to the car, they wouldn't fit in it. I was getting a bit stressed out, when suddenly, Gordon did something. I didn't see what. But the next thing I knew, they slid into the car with room to spare. It was as though he'd shrunk them somehow. I know that sounds daft."

"Couldn't it just be that he turned them around, and put them in a different way?" Greg suggested.

"No. We'd tried to put them in every which way, and they simply wouldn't fit. When I asked him how he'd done it, he just shrugged. When we got back home, and took them out of the car, they were back to their original size. It was just weird. And then, there was the time when we were walking down the street, and a young girl on a bicycle came flying past. She seemed to have lost control, and was headed straight for the busy road at the bottom of the hill. The next thing I knew, Gordon had rushed down the street, and caught her just before she reached the road."

"Surely that was just instinctive," Greg said.

"Of course it was. But there was no way he should have been able to catch up with her. One moment he was standing next to me, and the next, he was at the bottom of the road. He moved so fast he was a blur. There were other weird things, too. One day, he was working on the car. He'd crawled under it to do something to the exhaust. I was sitting outside in the sun when suddenly I heard the jack creak and give way. I screamed. I thought that was the end for Gordon, but somehow he managed to hold the car up, and crawl out unscathed."

"You do sometimes hear stories of people who find remarkable strength when something terrible happens," Susan said.

"But it wasn't like that. It took no effort at all for him to support the full weight of the car. I confronted him about it, and demanded to know what was going on. That's when he sat me down and told me the truth. I didn't know what to think. I mean, what would you think if your husband told you he was a wizard? I thought wizards only existed in books or films. But he insisted it was true, and that he actually came from another land—a place called Candlefield where all manner of paranormal creatures live. And to prove it, he showed me all kinds of magic until I had to accept that what he'd said was true. He told me I must never tell anyone because if the authorities back in Candlefield ever found out, they'd send people to take him back. 'Rogue Retrievers' he called them. Of course, I promised I'd never say anything, and I didn't. But somehow, the authorities must have found out because he was taken away from me."

"Did you actually see them take him?" Susan asked.

"No. I was visiting my sister at the time. I'd only been gone for a couple of hours, but when I came back, he'd gone. I thought at first he'd just gone out to the shops or was visiting friends. When night fell, and there was still no sign of him, I called the police, but they weren't interested. They said he was an adult, and that they couldn't do anything until he'd been missing for some time. I contacted them again a few days later, and they said the chances were he'd probably walked out, and that people left relationships all the time."

"Could that have been what happened?" Susan said.

"No. We were perfectly happy. There's no way he walked out on me. I'm absolutely sure he was taken by the Rogue Retrievers back to Candlefield. Gordon wasn't the only wizard living around here. He told me there are lots of paranormal creatures living here among us in Washbridge."

After they'd left Mary's house, Susan and Greg went for a drink in a pub just down the road.

"So?" Greg took a sip of his beer. "What did you make of that?"

"Her story is almost identical to the one Margie told me. In both cases, their husbands told them that they were wizards, and both men disappeared without a trace."

"Do you believe their stories?"

"To a point. I believe that the men disappeared, and probably didn't go voluntarily. I'm definitely keen to follow up on the missing person angle."

"What about the paranormal angle? Surely, you can't just dismiss that out of hand?"

"How can you expect me to believe that there are wizards, werewolves and vampires living here among us. That's just ridiculous."

"Why is it so ridiculous? You thought you had a ghost."

"I was just sleep deprived. Maybe it's just a case of mass delusion, I don't know. But paranormal? Definitely not."

Chapter 24

Early the next morning, Susan's phone rang. It was the call she'd been waiting for.

"Ray? What did you find?"

"They're a match. Now whose prints are they?"

"Meet me in Aroma in thirty minutes."

"Why can't you just tell me now?"

"I have a file that I need to give to you. It has all the information you'll need on all four murders."

"Okay, I'll be there."

Thirty minutes later, the two of them were in Aroma.

"So?" Ray couldn't hide his impatience. "Whose prints are they?"

"Robert Marks'."

"The councillor? The guy who's standing for election as MP?"

"None other."

"Are you sure?"

"Of course I'm sure."

"Does he have the tattoo?"

"Of a crab, you mean? No. There never was a tattoo of a crab."

"You're not making any sense, Susan. The guy who was murdered wrote 'Crab Tattoo' in his blood."

"I know. I believe that there were four young men in the pharmacy that night. One of them, Chris Briggs, used to work there before he was sacked. He may still have had a key. The pharmacist must have walked in on them while they were helping themselves to drugs. Marks hit him on the back of the head with a chair—that's why his fingerprints were on the chair leg. The man fell onto the glass cabinet, and severed an artery. While he was lying on the floor, he must have seen the legs of the four boys who were all wearing shorts. These four friends all had similar tattoos on their legs. A circle with their initial inside it: 'C' for Chris Briggs, 'R' for Richy or Richard Price, 'A' for Alan Charlton and 'B' for Bob Marks, as he was known back then. The dying man saw the four letters which spelt the word 'CRAB'."

"Why didn't he just write Briggs' name?"

"I don't know. Maybe they were wearing masks. He was flat out on the floor; the only thing he would have got a good look at was their legs."

"You said the murderer had killed four men?"

"Yes. Marks has ambitions to be an MP, so he couldn't afford for his past to come back and bite him in the bum. It was easy for him to get rid of his own tattoo. If you check, I'm sure you'll find that it's been removed by laser. It was more difficult to ensure the silence of the other three men. The only way to guarantee they didn't talk was to get rid of them permanently. He couldn't afford to do it all at one time. No matter how carefully he'd planned it, the death of three men in a short period of time would have sounded alarm bells. Instead, he played the long game. Firstly, four years ago, he killed Richard Price. I'm not sure exactly how he did it, but it was made to look like a road traffic accident. According to Price's widow, blood was found at the scene. Blood which did not match her husband's. My guess is that a DNA check will match it to Marks. Also, in this file you'll find an article that The Bugle ran about Marks which is dated two days after Price died. Marks appeared at a fundraising dinner with cuts and bruises to his head. At the time he said he had sustained the injuries when he fell from a ladder. I think it's more likely that they came from the car crash which he somehow orchestrated.

Then, two years ago, Alan Charlton died in a climbing accident. He was supposed to have been climbing with someone. There were actually witnesses who said they saw him with another man. But when his body was found, he was alone; there was no sign of his climbing companion. There's another article in this file from the Bugle taken from around the date that Charlton died. The reporters at The Bugle had been trying to get hold of Marks for a comment on a last minute, controversial change to the council's budget. They were unable to contact him because he was 'incognito'. According to his representative, Marks was on vacation, but no one seemed to know where. My guess is he was in the Peak District with Alan Charlton. If you can get hold of the witnesses who thought they'd seen someone with Charlton that day, I suspect they'll be able to identify that person as Marks.

And last, but not least, is poor old Chris Briggs. He supposedly committed suicide recently by jumping off the multi-storey car park. I have nothing to link Marks with his death, but I'd bet my life he was behind it. As a councillor, he had access to the fifth floor and roof of the car park directly from his offices. He could have taken Briggs up to the roof without it ever being caught on CCTV."

Her brother looked stunned. "This is going to take some time to check out."

"The story runs in The Bugle tomorrow."

"At least wait until we've had a chance to investigate it properly. Let the police do their job."

"The police have had ten years, Ray, and so far, nothing's come of it. I'm not going to wait because if I do, the story will get out, and all the other papers will run it. This is a big story for The Bugle, and we're going to break it first. It will be in tomorrow's edition."

"But if you're wrong—"

"I'm not."

When Susan got back to The Bugle, Flynn called her into his office. "Are you absolutely sure about this story?"

"Positive."

"If we run it and you're wrong, it'll be the end of this paper. You do realise that, don't you?"

"You've seen the file, Flynn. All the evidence is there. His fingerprints are on the chair—he killed the pharmacist, and most likely killed his three friends too."

Flynn took a deep breath. "Okay. We'll run it tomorrow."

Susan stayed late at the office, and before she left, picked up an early mock-up of the next day's paper. The headline was 'MP is Crab Tattoo Murderer.' The article focussed on the ten-year-old murder of the pharmacist for which there was the most compelling evidence. It mentioned the other deaths, but didn't make any direct accusations against Marks. The article was everything she'd hoped it would be, and more. If this didn't get The Bugle noticed for the right reasons, she didn't know what would.

As she left the office, she bumped into Tom Wallace.

"Why are you always hanging around here?" she said, accusingly.

"You do realise that my office is only two doors down?"

"Oh, right. No, sorry, I didn't."

"Anyway, I'm glad I've bumped into you," he said. "I thought you'd like to see our headline for tomorrow's paper. This is what a real newspaper is all about." He held up the early edition of In The Wash. The headline read: 'Police Chief Implicated in Extortion Racket.'

That immediately rang a bell with Susan. It was the story that Manic had tried to give to her. Had he taken it to Wallace? Had Wallace paid Manic?

"What do you think?" Wallace said. "Are you beginning to regret not joining us?"

"Not really." She opened her bag, and pulled out the mock-up of The Bugle.

"Read it and weep."

When he saw the headline, his face fell.

"See you around, Tom."

***

The next morning, the other three housemates were already in the lounge when Susan emerged from her bedroom after a well-deserved lie-in.

"I see you've got the big story you were hoping for." Neil was holding a copy of that morning's Bugle.

"Solved a murder and brought down Washbridge's would-be MP." Charlie flashed Susan that big smile of his. "I just heard on the radio news that Marks has been arrested. Congrats!"

"Not bad." Dorothy managed, rather less enthusiastically.

"Thanks, guys." Susan took a seat on the sofa next to Charlie.

"Your new bosses must be pleased with you," Charlie said.

"I guess so. Now all I have to do is find more stories like this one."

"Easier said than done, I imagine." Neil put the paper down.

"That's true. Still, if all else fails, I suppose I could always do a story on Margie, Mary, and the missing wizards."

The others looked at her in horror.

Susan laughed. "But then the men in white coats would have to come and take me away."

ALSO BY ADELE ABBOTT

The Witch P.I. Mysteries:

Witch Is When... (Books #1 to #12)
Witch Is When It All Began
Witch Is When Life Got Complicated
Witch Is When Everything Went Crazy
Witch Is When Things Fell Apart
Witch Is When The Bubble Burst
Witch Is When The Penny Dropped
Witch Is When The Floodgates Opened
Witch Is When The Hammer Fell
Witch Is When My Heart Broke
Witch Is When I Said Goodbye
Witch Is When Stuff Got Serious
Witch Is When All Was Revealed

Witch Is Why... (Books #13 to #24)
Witch Is Why Time Stood Still
Witch is Why The Laughter Stopped
Witch is Why Another Door Opened
Witch is Why Two Became One
Witch is Why The Moon Disappeared
Witch is Why The Wolf Howled
Witch is Why The Music Stopped
Witch is Why A Pin Dropped
Witch is Why The Owl Returned
Witch is Why The Search Began
Witch is Why Promises Were Broken
Witch is Why It Was Over

The Susan Hall Mysteries:

Whoops! Our New Flatmate Is A Human.
Whoops! All The Money Went Missing.
Whoops! Someone Is On Our Case.
See web site for availability.

AUTHOR'S WEB SITE
http:www.AdeleAbbott.com

FACEBOOK
http://www.facebook.com/AdeleAbbottAuthor

MAILING LIST
(new release notifications only)
http:/AdeleAbbott.com/adele/new-releases/